T0146923

Elwood Farm

FRIENDS IN DANGER

David Paul

Illustrations by Julian Collins

For book orders, email orders@traffordpublishing.com.sg

Most Trafford Singapore titles are also available at major online book retailers.

Printed in Singapore.

ISBN: 978-1-4907-0011-3 (sc)
ISBN: 978-1-4907-0012-0 (hc)
ISBN: 978-1-4907-0013-7 (e)

Trafford rev. 07/27/2013

Singapore
toll-free: 800 101 2656 (Singapore)
Fax: 800 101 2656 (Singapore)

List of Illustrations

Contents

Preface

"Learning is more our growth as friend Relationships
will shape our end"
David Paul, 'Invigilation in Memorial Hall', ll 29-30

The Author

The author was a retired teacher of History, English and Drama. This is his first published work but he has written eleven stories for and about his Grand-children, a Nativity Play and books of verse—some of which may yet be published.

The Story

These are the adventures of Emily and Sarah, two close friends who are in early secondary school. They see suspicious activity on Emily's father's farm and decide to investigate. The adventures that follow turn out to be more scary and dangerous than they could have imagined. The Gang is led by the clever 'Shelly' Beach—but is she clever enough to outwit the girls?

School-yard Language

The language of school children is both colourful and formalized. In *Book Two: The Return of the Gang,* I have included a section in which Emily and Sarah must use the language of the school-yard—something they do not use with each other. 'OMG' is "-Oh, My God", a statement of shock, horror or disgust. The overuse of the word 'like' seems to be required in each spoken sentence. I am indebted to Cathy Crick, who gave me the seal of approval on this section.

Dedication

The book is for Maeve, for her ideas for the story and for her encouragement after reading the final product—and simply because she's Maeve.

Acknowledgements

I would like to thank Julian Collins for his excellent line drawings and particularly that he agreed to do them at short notice and was so amenable to doing them in the way that I visualised the scenes.

I thank also my wife, Veida, who kept me alive long enough to write this and to prepare it for publication.

PART 1

The Girls & the Gang

The Girls See a Strange Boat Approaching the Farm Beach

Chapter One

The Farm and the Boat

Emily Wood sighed as she leant forward over her horse's neck and stared out at the water. She was still finding it difficult to decide whether she was happier where she was or whether she had been happier before her family had moved to the farm. She looked across at her friend, Sarah, and sighed again. It was at least a real bonus that her very best friend visited so often. Though they were both generally very chatty together, they were also comfortable in times of reflection, such as at this moment. Emily was quiet because she was thinking about the pros and cons of life away from Melbourne and on the farm.

On the one hand, the farm was on a very attractive stretch of land that ran in an L-shape along the cliffs above a beach that had millions of small pebbles among the sand. These pebbles came from stones in the cliff that had been tossed over and over in the surf at high tide until they had become soft and rounded. It was not surprising that the area of sand behind the rocks had been called Small Pebbles Beach.

The other side of the farm was a hilly area that intruded like a wedge into the farmland. The farm made an L-shape with cliffs on the long side and hill on the other. The family name was Wood, so Dad had called the farm *Elwood*.

Being on the farm, Emily could roam from hill to beach, although it had been made clear that the beach could be a dangerous place. She must never go alone into the water, not even the beautiful clear pool that was left in the rocks at low tide. She knew that with one slip she could hit her head and drown. Or a sudden wave could sweep her out to sea.

She loved just to sit near the cliff edge and watch the energy-of the he waves as they crashed on the rocks and sand as if they were angry and wanted to punish them.

She also liked the farm animals. She liked the fuss the hens made, especially in the evening when she went to feed them. They strutted around as if they were really important. Emily knew some people who reminded her of these hens. The man who ran the post office was exactly like that and she had even named a rooster after Mr Stretton.

Most successfully, Dad had won her over by bribery. He had bought her a horse, an oldish horse, although he preferred to call it 'experienced'. Its name was Pebbles. It was a lovely dark chestnut and it had gentle ways. The gentleness was very important for someone who had had little experience with horses.

Pebbles was named after the beach and an early experience it had there, when some pebbles had worked inside one of its shoes, a shoe that had come loose. Dad had removed the pebbles but not before Emily had decided that the horse should be called Pebbles.

Now Sarah had a horse too. Sarah's horse, a palomino, was a pale colour, almost beige. It seemed natural that with Emily's horse being Pebbles, Sarah would call her horse Sand. Most of the time Emily had to look after it, as Sarah still lived in Melbourne.

Emily had a dog, a small and rather scruffy animal, called Timmy because she had heard about a dog called Timmy that had been the hero in a story she had once read. This Timmy had saved its owner from all sorts of dangerous situations, from house fires and flooded rivers and nasty criminals. Secretly, Emily hoped that her Timmy would be like this, although in her heart she knew that this was just a story and that dogs could not think like that.

Finally, on the side of preferring the farm, she was slowly making friends at her new school. It was a process that took a great deal of patience. Friendship groups had been formed the year before and Emily was "the city girl". Emily was a determined friend-maker, however. Her response to this was a mixture of three things. She was persistently kind, she shared nice things with other girls and she had inherited her mother's easy good nature.

She still missed her old friends from Elsternwick. This was as a nice suburb of Melbourne that was handy to both the city centre and the beaches of Port Phillip Bay. Many primary school friends went to the same secondary school, where they were all in Year 8. Her parents and the parents of her best friend, Sarah, had got along really well and had even holidayed together.

In fact it was on one such holiday that her Dad had seen the farm's 'For Sale' sign and said that they should have a look. He had excitedly stuck his nose into everything and behaved rather like a three year-old on a chocolate hunt at Easter.

When Natalie, Emily's mother, drove back to the Snuggle Cove house, Graham, Emily-'s Dad, was quiet. Something was up. Even Emily's pesky little brother, Harry, could sense that something was different. It was clear that every-one felt uncomfortable about the situation.

Finally, Sarah's Dad, Crispin James, had broken the ice. "So you think you'll buy the farm, sell up in Melbourne and spend the rest of your life milking cows and cleaning out pig pens," he said. Dad simply turned around a little in his seat to face Crispin and said, "Yes. Probably. Something like that".

Emily remembered the feeling of the blood draining from her face and of a sick feeling in her stomach. He was serious. He was really thinking about buying the farm.

That night, with the children in bed, Graham had defended himself by saying that he had been feeling increasingly unhappy as a stockbroker. At 45 he had made sure they owned their house in Elsternwick, and he had a couple of investment properties, one in Ringwood and another, an apartment, in the city. If he sold Elsternwick and kept the other properties, he could not only buy the farm but he'd have money over. He would be free to work with his hands and see the results of that work instead of being stuck behind a computer screen all day.

Natalie had been happy with the decision. She was a homemaker. Although she would not be trampled on, belittled or ignored, she lived for Graham and the children and didn't care all that much for the city. She tolerated her book club but she had hated, and given up, the ladies' tennis days where women with solarium tans and designer dresses sniped at others and aired their husband's political prejudices. No, the change would be fine with her. It meant more time with Graham, and as a family.

"I would want to insist that you two and Sarah come and visit frequently," Graham had said to Crispin and Marion, his wife. We could do up the old cottage out the back; probably the original house." Marion, Sarah's mother, had at first thought the decision strange but she recognised that there were many advantages in Graham's plan and was soon won over. They all knew there should be good times ahead at the farm near Snuggle Cove.

Emily, who was not asleep, had heard it all and had started to weep quietly. Her world had seemed to be rapidly falling apart.

Now, on her horse on the cliffs above the sea, she was not so sure. She was in her twilight zone of liking and disliking the change. In fact it was becoming real twilight where they were. Soon they would have to go home to the farm but this was not too far on Pebbles and Sand; probably ten minutes.

She looked across at Sarah, who turned and smiled at her. To be honest, Sarah's frequent visits really tipped the scale in favour of the farm. She sighed again and looked out over the water. A boat was coming in toward the beach. It had a central mast with sails that two men on the boat were furling as the quiet, deep throated chug of a powerful motor took over from the sails. Emily wondered what it was doing coming in to their beach; and at that late time of the day. She shrugged at Sarah and they turned their horses around toward the farm, toward their families, their homework (Sarah had brought hers with her from Melbourne) and, more importantly, toward their dinner.

Chapter Two

A Clear Starry Night

Emily and Sarah agreed that they wouldn't tell their parents about the boat coming in to Small Pebbles Beach. They thought of it as their own private experience. They also thought that they might check it out again later if they finished their homework quickly and could sneak out. It looked as if it would be a clear night again. The night before this one had been nearly a full moon. It would be full in another day or two and without any clouds about it would be easy to see anywhere outside.

In the country it was so beautiful on a clear night. There was always pollution and a massive quantity of reflected street, house and car light hiding most of the stars in the city. Here it was so bright and starry on a night like this that it was almost as if you could climb a ladder and touch the stars on their black velvet mat. Emily had seen it many times in the months that they had been on the farm but the beauty of it still made her gasp.

First there was the evening meal and then she had to do her homework. There was the essay on whether or not duck shooting should be banned instead of just controlled. Of course there was always some Maths. Emily was clever and was enjoying the Algebra that many of the other children found such a struggle.

She now attended the Secondary School that serviced the older children of Snuggle Cove and Belton. Belton was the larger town, inland about fifteen minutes from Snuggle Cove and it catered for the local dairy industry and some of the children of the nearby Power Station workers. The diplomatic Emily would have to pretend in class that she did not know as much as she actually did. Her fellow students would have thought her to be a boastful person if they thought she knew it all. Emily did not want to be "-a smarty-pants", as it meant that she was smarter than was good for her.

After her Algebra which she found easy, she had to do some reading for the other subjects. She was also reading *Tomorrow When the War Began* by John Marsden. It was perhaps too old for her and she found some bits rather scary but she was a good reader.

Having done as much of her homework as was necessary, Emily picked up her book. The scary parts seemed even more so tonight, as she thought about what she and Sarah were about to do. What if they were seen? How would the strange people react if they knew they were being spied on?

Emily shuddered and closed her book. Perhaps she and Sarah were being silly doing what they had planned. Perhaps she should call the whole adventure off? Emily was no chicken but there was a difference between adventure and (what was the word?) foolhardiness.

She sat on the bed for a while in that state of indecision that makes you unable to do anything. Then she heard her mother's footsteps in the passage. She would be coming to check that Emily had finished her homework and was ready for bed.

Quickly she snatched up the book she had put down and curled up on the bed on her side, the book half falling from her hand. She realised as she lay there pretending to be asleep that what she was doing was making her decision. She would still go on the adventure with Sarah.

Emily had told Sarah that she would come and tap on her window but she had made the mistake of lying down to read the book. Tired from a long day's play and horse riding, she fell fast asleep. Her pretence had become reality.

At the cottage, Sarah also finished her homework, cleaned her teeth and put on her nightie. She was seen in bed by her mother when she came to turn out the light.

"Good night, Darling," said Marion.

"Good night, Mum," said Sarah.

Sarah snuggled down. She was going to pretend to sleep because she was getting ready in her mind to go out with Emily. Soon, however, sleep took control and she was gone into slumberland, dreaming of boats coming in to shore and strange people geting out. In her dreamy imagination they were smugglers from the olden days, bringing rum and pieces of eight (whatever they were) and hiding from the customs men. These officers would have tried to force taxes on their goods or would have captured them and thrown them into prison for their smuggling crime.

The smugglers were smart, however, and nearly always outwitted the bumbling customs men who were just one step behind them at any crisis moment.

Chapter Three

From Beach to Bush

Emily woke with a start. Did she hear something? Or was it just her imagination working on the plan that she had made to go with Sarah to check up on the boat at Small Pebbles Beach? Whatever woke her, she was wide awake and yet the clock beside her bed showed the time to be 11.30 p.m. She felt as if she'd had a night's sleep and yet it could only have been at best three to three and a half hours.

She jumped to her feet. She could see how bright it was outside; the stars shone and the moon rode in the middle of the sky.

"Perfect," she thought. "I can ride and still see where I'm going."

Emily tip-toed to the back door of the house, where she collected her riding boots. She let herself out quietly. Her parents were both sound asleep. Country life was working well for both of them. They were physically active during the day and slept well at night. Her mother's face looked more relaxed and she was calmer than she had been in years.

Emily remembered her musings of the afternoon and realized that whatever she might think of the move, it had worked for her parents and there was no going back. She would probably attend university in Melbourne; but they would not live—here as a family again.

She saddled Pebbles and walked him to the cottage. Crispin and her Dad had done a good job restoring it. It was the perfect weekender. She tied Pebbles lightly to a small gum and picked her way carefully to the window of the small bedroom that Sarah occupied. The blind of her room was not pulled down as far as it would go and Emily peeked through.

She tapped on the window, hoping that the noise would wake her without waking her parents and was pleased when Sarah sat bolt upright in bed and stared around with eyes that at first looked frightened. Then, as the sleep started to drop away from her, Sarah realized that it must have been Emily and she hurried across to the window and opened it a little.

"What time is it?" she asked sleepily.

"About midnight," was the reply.

Sarah yawned. She was slower to wake up than Emily had been but she dressed and joined her friend. She was not going to miss out on an adventure. Like Emily she had become more than a little nervous. But if Emily could head off in the middle of the night, on a scary adventure, then she could too.

Emily helped her saddle Sand who nuzzled her softly and shook her mane. Sarah smiled, realizing how much she already loved a horse she had owned for less than six months. Sand had a nice even gait and seemed to understand that she could not be too adventurous with speed. She fell into an easy rhythm that Sarah could quickly adapt to.

The two friends trotted easily to the cliffs overlooking Small Pebbles beach. There, bobbing gently, was the boat they had seen in the late afternoon. Three people were near the waterline, and the girls watched them pull a cart with fat tyres up the beach towards the track through the east paddock of the farm.

Emily and Sarah gasped at the figures on the beach. Who were they? What were they doing with a laden cart on the beach and heading for the east paddock? Emily slid off her horse and Sarah quickly dismounted as well. When the three from the beach reached the paddock, they would have been seen, high on their horses and silhouetted against the sky

They pulled the horses into what Emily had discovered was the old beach track. The cliff had been eroded over the years and of the beach below. It made a good hiding place, hiding from the people who were so brazenly using their farm as a track to—where? And why?

Emily looked at Sarah who was asking herself the same questions. The two girls were so close that they did not always need to say what both thought on a particular point. They called it telepathy but it was more a function of long and close friendship. They knew each other better than many married couples achieve in an adult lifetime together.

They held their horses' reins tightly. They watched as the strange group of three hauled their precious cargo across the paddock. From the way they walked, Emily could see there must be two males and a female. Emily wondered whether they should go back to the farm buildings and wake their parents.

They didn't, however: they still felt this was their own pesonal adventure and, besides, they could easily lose the intruders if they took time out to go back. They were moving quite quickly now and seemed to know exactly where they were going. Emily guessed that they had already been there that night. This was by no means their first trip with the cart to somewhere in the bush.

They were excited now and the adrenalin rush of excitement took over, to some extent, from the fright. Or perhaps the fright was a large part of the excitement. It was like seeing a really scary movie. The difference was that they were actually *in* this movie, not watching it safely from a seat in a cinema.

Clearly, the three were up to no good. But how could they have had such intimate knowledge of the beach and farm? As they watched, the group crossed the east field and disappeared into the bush at the bottom of the hill.

Slowly the two girls came out of their hiding place and started back across the farm. Curiosity took over from fright. They just had to know what was going on. They decided that they would quietly follow the group, spy on them and see what they were up to.

The Gang Bury Stolen Goods

Chapter Four

Capture

As the girls reached the edge of the hill, they dismounted. At first they wondered whether they would leave the horses at the bottom and walk up, since the horses would be easier to see than two smallish girls and Sand, in particular, would be easy to see with her light colour. Sarah argued,—however, that if they were seen they might want to escape in a hurry and the horses would be a quicker way to escape than on foot if they were being chased by grown men.

It had seemed a reasonable argument at the time, although they could not have known that it would not work out too well in practice. When they looked back on it later, they realized that they had been rather silly to have been out in the dark, climbing a hill in pursuit of suspicious characters all by themselves when their parents thought they were safely tucked up in bed. They wouldn't be missed until the morning.

Yes, later on they could look back and be very sensible indeed; but they were not too sensible at the time, walking up the steep hill with their horses and a small dog, heading towards unknown danger.

It was darker in there as well, as the height and density of the gums and the melaleuca obscured, to some extent, the brightness of the night that had so appealed to Emily on the clear land of the farm. Emily could feel herself starting to perspire—perhaps rather more than the climb up the hill could have explained. If it was adventure they were after, they were certainly having it. Sarah was feeling increasingly nervous as well but she was not going to admit to Emily that she had any doubts. Emily, at least on the surface, seemed to be so calm.

Suddenly Emily stopped and grabbed Sarah's arm. Through the trees about 50 metres away she had seen a light. Sarah saw it at almost the same time. She took a nervous gulp of air and stood still. Her legs began to shake so much that she began to wonder if she could actually run to the horses if they were discovered.

"We'd better leave the horses here," she whispered to Emily. "We can't risk them any closer."

Emily nodded her agreement. They tied the horses up, but loosely so that they could be easily untied in an emergency. Then they crept carefully and slowly toward the light. Sarah felt that her heart must be pounding so loudly that the strangers must surely have heard it but they were so intent on their task and so sure that they were alone that they did not look up.

They were putting boxes wrapped in plastic bags in to a hole in the ground. The girls noticed that some bushes had been dug up, roots and all, and that the hole was under where the bushes had been. Two large and solid folding doors were open, as if the hole was a large cellar. It was a cellar, in a kind of way, but instead of being a store for something like wine, expensive electronic equipment, like TVs and DVD players, laptop computers and boxes of mobile phones were being fastened carefully in strong orange plastic bags, like garden tidy bags, to keep them dry.

Another provision was a thick tarpaulin to be placed over the folding doors before the bushes, as camouflage, were replaced, disguising the presence of anything there other than the bushes themselves. Emily couldn't help admiring the obvious thieves who had chosen their spot very carefully. The cellar had been dug on a gentle slope, with a strong plastic drainage channel on the high side and down each side.

The tarpaulin would be tucked into the drain and any rain that fell would water the bushes above and then run away down the drain instead of going in to the cellar.

The thieves, two men and a woman, seemed to have thought of everything, except perhaps that two fourteen year-old girls might come spying on them. Emily and Sarah turned to each other and, as if at a signal, put their fingers to their lips and indicated the need for them to retreat. They had seen enough. They could creep down the hill and back to the farm, wake their parents and get them to call the police. No matter how well these three had planned and executed their little scheme, they had been found out All that was needed was that the girls should get away unknoticed.

They had turned and started moving when disaster struck. Pebbles was obviously uncomfortable about being left tied up in the bush at night. Perhaps he simply wanted to indicate to Emily that the night time was for sleeping in his comfortable stall in the hay, with his feed bag handy for a little grazing if he felt hungry. For whatever reason, he whinnied loudly and Sand, who clearly shared his opinion, followed suit. The thieves whirled around and the two men came crashing through the undergrowth in pursuit of the fleeing girls who were stumbling along, as their legs had seemed to turn to jelly with fright.

They weren't even very close to the horses when they were run to earth and thrown roughly to the ground so that their faces and arms were scratched. They shrieked, which spooked the horses even more. They rose on their hind legs and whinnied even more loudly, shook off the loose tie on the bushes and galloped off down the hill, crashing through foliage as they went. Timmy yelped with fright and tore off after them.

The male thieves, each one of which was holding down a struggling girl, pursed their lips in annoyance. Fully saddled horses would draw attention to the fact that the girls had been out. The horses' legs, scratched by sticks would suggest the hill. The gang might have captured the intruders but their secret hiding place could be quickly compromised by the search that would follow the discovery of the saddled horses and the absence of their riders.

"Damn ya," snarled the bigger of the two, who had hold of Emily. "What did ya 'ave t' come round snoopin' at a time when ya should be safely tucked up in bed?"

Emily was blubbing uncontrollably. She had been asking herself the same question. She had never been so frightened in her life, even at the time when she was eight when her father saved her from drowning in rough surf. He had not been too far away and he had acted quickly. He was nowhere near her now. She had seen to that with her secrecy.

What a fool she had been! The adventure was now a nightmare. They could easily pay for this stupidity with their lives. Surely the thieves could not let the girls go. If they did their hiding place was no longer any use. If they were alive, the thieves could be identified as being the ones responsible. Emily began to shriek with fear.

"Shut up or I'll shut ya up," menaced her captor, raising his hand to strike her. Emily reduced the volume of her fear by ninety percent as she could see that he meant it and she did not want to be struck. She whimpered quietly instead. By contrast, Sarah was quiet and still. This did not mean she was being brave, much less that she was happy with her situation. She was in fact struck dumb with fear. She shook uncontrollably while the other man leant roughly on her back.

The woman wandered over to the place of capture. She was quiet, as she was clearly thinking furiously about what course of action they would take.

"What d'ya reckon we do with 'em, Shelly?" asked the bigger man. Shelly was clearly the one in charge. Her name was actually Fiona Beach, but it doesn't take a great deal of imagination to see why she was called "Shelly". The men provided the muscle, or in particular, the bigger one did. He was large and muscular, with an unattractively bell-shaped head. The precise role of the smaller one was not immediately clear. Shelly looked annoyed.

"Well, we can't let them go," she replied. "Certainly not before this hideaway has served its purpose. And that could take months," she added. "Killin' them's a bit drastic but it might be necessary". She was thinking aloud.

The girls' fear was not improved by what she said. Months of capture. Or death? Even the first alternative was unthinkable'; the second one so bad that they could not, dare not, think of it as a reality. What was more, they knew that people *were* actually murdered by criminals, by people who were not normal in society but rather anti-social, unhinged, flawed or simply greedy.

The girls knew it was not an easy thing for a normal person to actually murder someone who is not immediately threatening his or her life or causing long-term aggravation. Most murders occur within families and even gangster in-fighting can be defined as a form of family. It usually involved complicated rivalries within a community of villains. Even the killing of hostages in very poor counties by bandit and rebel groups, is not as common as TV shows would suggest. While they knew this, they nevertheless felt anything but safe. They were a risk to the gang and as such they were vulnerable.

Shelly knew how useful the threat of violence would be on these young girls who were already frightened. She also had the perfect weapon in the smallest member of her gang, Billy Oakshott, nick-named "One-Shot". The origin of the name was not clear. Some said he was so deadly that he took only one shot to make his kill. Others said he had only ever fired one shot. These people argued that even that shot had missed its intended taget. Whatever the story, "One Shot" had a hand gun, was fond of showing it and enjoyed seeing the fright it and the nick-name created in people he was dealing with.

"Show them your weapon, One-Shot," said Shelly, to reinforce the point.

One-Shot grinned, reached behind his back and picked what first seemed a toy hand gun from his belt. It was black, with a sloping handle that fitted the fingers for a better grip. The magazine protruding from the handle showed it to be other than a toy. One-Shot ejected it with an expert flick and showed the rounds of ammunition inside.

"Glock 9 millimetre," he muttered. "Seventeen rounds. One fer the barrel and sixteen in the magazine." He thrust the magazine back with a sharp click while the girls looked on in wide-eyed horror. They found

it impossible to stop their teeth chattering. Shelly looked on in grim amusement. "That should keep them quiet." She mouthed to herself. "They're not likely to try to run away now-."

The big man, who looked to be more muscle than brain, spoke. "-What d'ya want us to do now, Shelly?" he asked.

"Let's get the last box in the ground and tidy the place up," she answered. "And then let's get out of here before the people down below find the horses and send out a search party. We've got to be back on the boat in about half an hour, I'd say, for safety. Unless the horses make a noise and wake them up, we've probably got until about dawn."

"Farmer could be up a fair while before dawn. If he's milkin'," said One-Shot knowingly. Clearly he knew something about farming, which Emily thought strange for someone who appeared to be entirely a city person. Shelly smiled but said only:

"Let's get on with it. Bring the girls back to the hiding place and tie them to a tree. Better gag them as well."

Emily said, "No, please don't gag us. I promise—absolutely promise—that I won't call out. I have trouble breathing through my nose. I'll die if that's covered. You can shoot me if I break my promise."

"You bet yer life I will," snarled One-Shot.

"What about you, Blondie?" asked Shelly.

"My name's Sarah and this is Emily," said Sarah, feeling vaguely silly that she was making what sounded like formal introductions with desperate criminals. "But, yes, I promise not to call out as well. I don't particularly want to be shot by this . . . gentleman", she finished lamely, not knowing what else to call him.

The three couldn't help grinning at the thought of One-Shot as a gentleman.

"Come on, Shady," said One-Shot eventually, "Let's get the job done.

The girls assumed that 'Shady' was a description of the big one's character, but Shady Jenkins had actually been named after the persistent 'six o'clock shadow' of stubbly black hair that could be seen on his face all day and all night; in fact for all but an hour or two in the morning after shaving.

The two men worked quickly to cover the final box, what looked like DVDs, and stack it carefully in the hole. Then they shut the doors on their frame, threw the tarp over and fixed the sides in-the drain before covering it with a double thickness of shade cloth which, being porous, would allow water to run through. They quickly replaced the shrubbery piling earth around their root balls and throwing damp leaves and twigs over the earth. When they'd finished, in less than ten minutes, you would swear the area had never been disturbed, much less guess at what actually lay beneath.

The girls couldn't help a gasp of admiration.

"Yes, clever, isn't it? All my own idea," Shelly boasted. "-The cops suspect the warehouse haul was our work and they know all the usual places we might have stored the stuff. The people who might have looked after it for us got too greedy so I came up with a new idea: van to country dock by night, boat to here."

"But how did you know about this place?" gasped Emily.

"Don't ask no more questions than what is good for ya," snarled Shady, whose meaning was clearer than his grammar was accurate. "Ya don't want t'have sleepin' dogs barkin' up the wrong tree," he added.

Shelly smiled. Shady was useful in that he knew his limitations and was not likely to act out of line, knowing that he would probably get things wrong. His other great strengths were his brawn—he was built like an ox—and the fact that he was an excellent driver and handy car mechanic. He'd got them out of more than one scrape in the past.

One-Shot had met him in prison, when Shady had saved him from some prison thugs who had been terrorising him. Shady had a good nature, like many very strong men, and he had thought the thugs were being unfair to the little man. In gratitude, One-Shot would now do anything for him and the two had become firm friends.

Chapter Five

At the Beach

The move to the beach was quite quick. Clearly the three electronics thieves were entirely familiar with the area and knew the quickest way from beach to bush and from bush to beach. The girls had their hands tied behind their backs and had no other restraints, so they could walk quite quickly as they were required to do.

As they moved across the farm land, Emily felt a tug of attachment to the paddocks and the more or less distant glimpse of the farm house where, had she been wiser, she could now have been tucked up safely in her warm and comfy bed. She glanced at Sarah and noticed that she was thinking much the same thing. A sad and wistful look crossed her face and a slow drawing-in of breath was clearly a substitute for bursting into tears.

Going down the new track to the beach was like being condemned to turn their backs on safety, as they were about to be obliged to board the boat with their three captors.

"Sit down there on the sand," ordered Shelly, "While we go off shore to get the boat ready to sail."

To reinforce the order, the girls were pushed roughly on to the sand, where they were told to, "-Sit still, or else!" What the "Or else" was they could easily imagine.

Shelly and Shady hopped into a little snub-nosed dinghy that had rowlocks (rounded metal oar rests) but no motor. Without a motor the dinghy made almost no noise as it slupped gently through the water out to the yacht, carrying Shady, Shelly and the trolley.

Back on the beach, Sarah had become very quiet. Emily was wriggling a little, trying to be more comfortable while her wrists swelled from the twine that held them together. One-Shot was sitting on a nearby rock having a cigarette, in fact several cigarettes.

He was a rather nervy individual and obviously quite addicted. He was watching the boat out on the water, wishing he was out there with them, instead of sitting on an uncomfortable rock on the beach being a mixture of jailor and baby-sitter.

To make matters worse, the weather was changing. Dark clouds were now covering the bright moon and a wind was getting up, making One-Shot shiver and stare even more longingly at the yacht, now rocking uncomfortably on the dark sea. The beach had become obscured by shadows and beach detail was less visible.

Then Sarah gave a little, almost inaudible, sound of triumph. Only Emily could see that she had freed her hands and was wriggling quietly towards her. Emily turned her back on her, so that she could be freed in turn. When this had been achieved, Emily put her finger to her lips and crawled down the beach, with Sarah just behind. Soon they were on the edge of the rock pool.

"Follow me," she whispered. "Don't be afraid. Trust me."

Without taking off even her shoes, Emily slipped gently into the water and Sarah, after a moment's hesitation, did the same. Emily took a deep breath, and Sarah copied her. They both went under the water, Emily holding Sarah's hand and gently pulling her along. Just as Sarah thought her lungs might burst, Emily rose in the water and Sarah found herself above the surface but in an air pocket, a little cave above the rock pool's watery surface. There was even a tiny crack in the rock ceiling above them, which let in fresh air.

Sarah gasped with appreciation and admiration. Here they were safe. The criminals would never find them, could never suspect that they could be there. As they would see it, the girls must have run along the beach and climbed the cliffs, making for the safety of the farm house. It would have been the obvious thing to do. One-Shot would chase after them, cursing his carelessness in allowing them to escape and expecting at any moment to run them to earth. When he could not find them, he would be forced to hurriedly call the boat. Their treasure would be lost, as the girls would tell the police, but perhaps they could escape capture.

The girls hugged each other with delight and then thought a little more about where they were. Only two things were wrong with their hiding place. They were already beginning to feel a bit cold. If forced to stay under water for an hour or more to make sure the three had gone, they would be really freezing, even past the teeth-chattering stage.

The other was that the rock pool was, of course, tidal. It was such a nice pool and such a great place to swim because twice a day the incoming tide washed over it, cleaning out the old water as waves crashed over its surface.

How long would they have before the water level rose as the tide did? How long would they have before the air space they were enjoying disappeared? It was fairly low tide when they slipped in to the pool, but they could not be sure whether the tide was still on the way out or whether it was already coming in again.

Sarah looked at Emily and could just make out her features with the help of dim light through the tiny crack. With a flat hand starting at the present water level she raised the hand up past their eyes to indicate the effects of a rising tide. Emily nodded. She understood that they had limited time. Both girls could only hope that their captors would give up looking for them fairly quickly. They could not survive for too long where they were, effective though the hiding place may be in the short term.

About half an hour later they thought they could hear the welcome sound of the motor on the boat starting up. Scarcely able to stop their teeth chattering with the cold, they breathed a sigh of relief. Obviously the criminals had given up the hunt and they would now be safe to come out. With Emily leading the way they sank down in to the water and swam back to the main part of the pool.

The tide was in fact on the way in as well, so there was not too much time to spare anyway. They dragged themselves shivering out of the pool and on to the rocky edge before standing up and moving on to the sand.

"Thank goodness," said Sarah, "I'm so cold that it's going to be an effort getting back to the farm."

"I can save yer that effort, Sarah," said an unwelcome voice from just behind them. "Ya can jist wait here with me until the boat comes back."

The girls gasped with horror. There, with his gun in his hand, was One-Shot, grinning at them in triumph and a very unpleasant grin it was.

"But," gasped the distraught Emily, "How did you know where we were? I thought we would be safe in the pool because nobody could know about the water cave."

"Not many would know about it, would they?" replied One-Shot in a nasty tone of voice. "Yer'll have ta excuse me, though, and wait fer the explanation while I make a little call to the boat. It's just reached the other side of the headland to be out of sight fer yer magical reappearance."

One-Shot made the call quickly, keeping the gun where he could access it easily if the girls made the silly decision of trying to rush him. All he said into the phone when it was answered the other end was, "They're out. Come an' get us."

"Now fer yer explanation," he said. "And what a pity yer so cold an' shivery! Serve ya right fer tryin' to escape," he added nastily. "Anyway, I knows about the pool and its little cave the same way I knows about the beach, the track t' the hill, the farm an' the hill itself. I were brought up 'ere in the little cottage yer've probably turned in to a flash weekender. Pretty small an' ordinary it was too in them days. Me father was the main farm hand fer old Mr Lowry who owned the place then. Me Mum used to do some washin' and ironin' fer the farmer's wife—snooty bitch, Ma Lowry—treated us like we was animals . . . . Maybe yer folks is like that too."

One-Shot's mouth had become a tight line and his eyes had glazed with the memory. Emily and Sarah were about to spring to the defence of their parents but thought better of it. One-Shot continued:

"I was real crook on meself when I'd found yez was gone, but I knew ya couldn't of gone far. Anyway, when I couldn't see ya when I'd run ta the top of the hill I guessed ya'd got smart an '-it the water. Ya tracks ta the pool edge was the clincher."

Emily and Sarah hadn't thought about the tracks they'd have left in their hurried escape. They didn't feel so clever now and to make matters worse they were still shivering with the cold.

Then they heard the chug of the boat, before the sound suddenly stopped as the boat engine was cut and it glided in toward the shore to avoid unnecessary noise. The tide was coming in all the time and the ends of waves were now washing over the rock pool. They could not have stayed in there much longer in any case, but it seemed cruel that they had seemed safe only to be found so easily

Chapter Six

The Return Trip

Shelly was far from amused when she had guided the dinghy in to the shore, as Shady stayed with the boat, expertly holding it steady though nearer to the shore than before. She fretted about the valuable lost time. They had to be away from this beach and back at the jetty where the vehicles were parked well before dawn and the girls' escape had lost them nearly an hour.

It was 3.00 a.m. The trip back to the jetty was a good two hours, maybe more with the tide running so strongly. They would have to travel a fair way by sail, which the boat was built for, having a fairly small fuel tank. They had needed extra space for their cargo and lacked space for spare fuel cans on the outward trip.

By the time Shelly reached the beach she was in a foul temper. She should have been most angry with One-Shot, whose careless watching was to blame but she needed him onside. The girls were the spies, the girls were the escapees and they must pay. She grabbed them roughly, banging their heads together. They felt sick, their heads ached and they saw stars. Shelly pointed roughly to the dinghy:

"Thought you'd be smart, did you?" she snarled. "We'll see how smart you are. Now get in and be very quiet."

The girls hurried to obey. Their future was on a knife edge. One further foiled escape and they'd be dead, their bodies probably weighted with an anchor and dropped well out to sea, where they might never be recovered.

Once on the boat they were pushed roughly in to the empty sail locker and the door slammed shut. The space was cramped and uncomfortable. It was not designed for passenger comfort. Though deep, to accommodate long sails, it was not high enough for the girls to be able to stand upright. The floor was hard and ucomfortable too and it was stuffy.

The only advantage was that they started to dry off and gradually the violent shivering became less frequent before stopping altogether. Another problem occupied them, however. Under sail, the boat tacked to and fro. The wind that was helping Shelly and the gang move fairly quickly through the water also made the surface very uneven.

As the boat pitched and tossed, Sarah, in particular, felt very sea-sick. The cramped condition of the sail locker did not help and the relatively airless atmosphere made Sarah gag. Eventually she was sick, violently and repeatedly sick. Emily also gagged with the boat's motion and the smell.

Nearing the landing jetty, both girls were very conscious of how exhausted they were. They had managed little sleep in their anxiety to have their great adventure, the adventure that had become a nightmare. They had been frightened out of their wits by capture and threats of death. They had dived into the rock pool, hidden in the cold and surfaced only to be captured again. They had headaches from their heads being banged together and they had been trussed like animals and thrown into a stuffy sail locker for the rough trip back. Now they had been sick and had ended up dry-retching from an empty stomach.

-When the boat had been tied up at the jetty, One-Shot came to get the prisoners He reeled back when he opened the sail locker.

"Oh, phew, disgusting!" he said as he smelt the vomit. "Don't yous have any control? Somebody—and it'll surely be me—has to clean all that up before we puts the sails away."

He swore loudly and repeatedly until Shelly came down to see what was happening. She looked at the mess, at the white-faced, frightened girls and she almost felt sorry for them—except that she reminded herself that they had brought it all on themselves, that they were a nuisance and a threat to the success of their enterprise.

"Get out and come with me," she ordered roughly. "One-Shot, you're going to have to clean this mess up before we put the sails away."

"I knew it," swore One-Shot. "Who else?"

"Shady's getting' the vehicles," said Shelly. "I'm going to look after these pests until I decide what to do with them. We'd a been back long ago if you'd watched 'em better. Then they mightn't've been so tired and got so sick."

One-Shot knew he deserved the punishment of the clean-up so he simply swore again loudly and went to get a mop, some rags and a bucket of water.

Shelly pushed the girls roughly to the ladder that led to the deck and then went up ahead of them. Shady had a van and a car, engines running, waiting on the road to the jetty.

"Throw them in the boot," snarled Shelly. "That way they'll be out of sight and they've promised not to call out if we happen to be stopped."

The girls groaned as they were heaved in to the large boot of the car, still with their hands bound. Their wrists were in pain now, from the tight bands. Their captors were taking no chances that Sarah could wriggle out as she had on the beach. They lay miserably in the dark when the boot lid was slammed down on them.

The little convoy set off. Shady drove the van and One-Shot the car, with a grim Shelly in the passenger seat beside him. When they reached Shelly's house they still had the problem of what to do with the girls. Shelly had not said so, but she had decided that they must not be killed—unless all else failed.

Jail for the theft of electronic goods was a chance she was prepared to take. It would be a relatively light sentence compared with the callous killing of young girls. By all means let them suffer a bit for their stupidity but even unlawful detention would be less serious than murder if they were found out.

They had reached the cross roads where they would turn off towards the city when they were stopped by a police car containing two policemen.

Chapter Seven

The Hunt is On

Officer Hutchinson was one of the policemen. He was tall and lean, with dark hair. Although he did not have the looks of a model, the girls generally found him attractive. It was a matter of his generally sunny temperament and a flashing smile that lit up his whole face. It was generally considered that he was on the way up in the police force and he expected that soon he would become a sergeant. He had recently become engaged to a very attractive girl whose large dark eyes had completely captivated him.

Hutchinson was on the look-out for the thieves who had broken into an electronics warehouse and stolen a large number of expensive items. Since a little earlier that morning he had been instructed also to keep an eye out for two young teenage girls, following the discovery at Elwood farm that Emily and Sarah were missing.

The alarm had been raised after Graham had risen early in the morning and found Pebbles and Sand grazing, fully saddled, outside the farm house. A frantic search had ensued with the absence of Emily raising their worst fears.

Timmy and the horses were no great help. Unlike the hero of the story, this Timmy just cowered on his bed, remembering his fright.

Where could she be? Sarah was obviously with her, as Sand was there, still saddled up as well. Nicole tore over to the shack, hoping that both girls would be there, perhaps asleep in Sarah's bed after a sneaky night ride adventure. But the girls would never have left the horses saddled!

Nicole and Marion were devastated to find that both the girls were missing. Had they been thrown from the horses that may have taken fright at some shadow, or a fox or possum suddenly on the path in front of them?

A frantic search of farm, beach and hill track followed without any sign of the girls. In near hysteria, Marion had phoned the police for help. No, they did not know exactly how long they had been missing; sometime after 10.00 p.m. the previous night and before 5.30 a.m. when Graham had risen to milk the cows.

No, they did not know exactly what they were wearing, but they would have had riding boots and a helmet each. Yes, she was sure about that because the girls were not allowed to ride without a helmet and the helmets were missing, anyway—and the riding boots.

The police had taken a description of the girls and had asked Marion to go to the nearest police station with recent photographs. They argued that it might be a good idea to have the media issue an alert. Clearly the girls had not just run away, as they had taken only what they had on. Nicole and Marion had searched the girls' wardrobe and now had an accurate description of what they would be wearing.

They had done what could be done and now came the worst part, waiting helplessly while the alarms had been put out. Nicole had initially felt inclined to blame Graham but she knew this was not fair. She had in fact felt safer at the farm than in Melbourne. Children could go missing there too, and sometimes did and when that happened the outcomes were almost always tragic.

Was it any better here, though? Some sort of foul play must have occurred for the girls to go missing so completely without any trace or clue as to a riding accident. Who could have taken them and how? Girls, in particular, were so vulnerable to predators. They dared not think what might have happened to them.

Chapter Eight

Strange Cargo

Officer Hutchinson peered carefully in the window of the car One-Shot was driving. "Who have we here and where are you going-?" he asked. "Well, look who it is! My old mate One-Shot Oakshott, if I'm not mistaken. And who's that next to you?" he added. "Shelly Beach, isn't it? What are you doing here? And isn't that Shady Jenkins in the van? Smells like trouble to me."

"Not at all, Officer Hutchinson," replied Shelly, "Just ordinary citizens out for a quiet drive on this beautiful early morning. You can't arrest us for that."

"True," replied Hutchinson. "At least it's true that we can't arrest you without evidence for what I seriously suspect has been your robbery of an electronics store. I'll just look in the back of the van, if you don't mind."

"Go right ahead," said Shelly, relieved that nothing would be found there. "Help yourself. Here, I'll open the back of the van for you."

Hutchinson and another policeman looked in the back of the empty van. Clearly there was no joy there in terms of evidence of stolen goods.

Officer Hutchinson scratched his dark head. There was nothing in the van beyond a few tarpaulins and some rope—not exactly illegal goods. He would have liked to look in the boot of the car but for that he needed reasonable suspicion and at the moment there was no excuse to do so.

"All right, all right," he said loudly so that the occupants of both vehicles could hear him. "That's it, then. Better be on your way—and don't forget that we'll be keeping an eye on you!" The gang members grinned with relief. It was working. The goods-were hidden and the girls had been frightened into silence.

In the boot, Emily and Sarah could hear what was going on outside. They were in despair. They had promised not to call out and yet they knew that their best hope of rescue was the policeman who had pulled their captors up. What could they do?

Suddenly, just as One-Shot was putting the car into gear, and as Officer Hutchinson was beginning to turn away towards his police vehicle, Emily turned herself over and gave the lid of the boot a heavy kick and then another.

Sarah understood what was happening and she lashed out too.

"I only said I wouldn't call out," said Emily to Sarah. "I didn't promise that I wouldn't kick."

"Go, Emily!" said Sarah. "What a great call!

Officer Hutchinson pulled his police weapon out from his belt. "Hold it, One-Shot", he shouted. "Stop the car and get out of it! You too, Shelly," he added.

The two groaned with despair. They had been thwarted when they had so nearly got away with it. Their goods would be discovered in their otherwise perfect hiding place. Prison would be the reward for all their efforts and their cleverness—and all because of two stupid girls who had interfered with their plans by spying on them.

One-Shot revved the car and it leapt forward, tearing down the road. Shady did the same with his van tyres shrieking. Soon they were near city streets, a noisy convoy with police cars, their sirens blaring, tearing along behind the feeing criminals. But it was not an escape that could last. To avoid stopping at an intersection, One-Shot ignored a red light. With a horrible crashing noise, a car going with the lights was struck behind the back door and whirled around, its frightened owner unhurt but looking as if he was sure he'd die.

One-Shot ended up in the gutter, loose because he was not wearing his seat belt. His car ended up against a lamp-post. Shelly was still sitting, but bruised, in the damaged front of the car. Shady screeched to a halt to avoid crashing into the wrecked cars, the police jumped from their vehicles and the criminals were soon handcuffed.

The boot was opened and the badly bruised, frightened and bedraggled girls were pulled out. They felt dreadful and overjoyed at the same time. They were an amusing sight to an outsider: black and blue, hair in knots, pasty faces, salt-encrusted and in dirty clothing that was a mixture of sand, greasy locker residue and vomit. You could hardly say that they were ready for the School Formal! Even the most careless adventurous boys on holiday at a piggery could not have been dirtier than they were. Yet they were grinning with relief. Emily wanted to hug the policeman but he backed off and who could blame him?

The police had been sent to the jetty because a nearby retired farmer who enjoyed looking out to sea in the evening with binoculars had watched as three doubtful characters had loaded a boat with goods the evening before and had now returned to their vehicles with an apparently empty boat. He had not seen the new cargo—the girls—but he had alerted the police. This situation had led to Officer Hutchinson and the other policeman waiting for the returning suspects.

The police had found rather more than they had expected when they apprehended the gang members, however. Strange cargo indeed!

"Don't worry," said Hutchinson kindly to the girls. "I'll soon have you home. Emily and Sarah burst into floods of tears from all their pent-up emotion and from relief.

"Home can't be that bad," Hutchinson said.

Chapter Nine

Reunion

The reunion of the girls with their parents was a highly emotional one but not exactly as the girls had expected it would be. They could see joyous and weeping mothers sweeping them up in their arms and kissing them until they felt overwhelmed with the love that was coming their way.

The reality was somewhat different. Their mothers were tearful, yes, but they were very angry as well.

"What have I told you Emily, about going *anywhere* without telling me? How could you have gone off into the night, on a horse that could have stumbled in the dark and thrown you? To . . . to spy on some dangerous criminals who could have, who nearly did, finish you off with a bullet to the brain . . . ?"

Just as it seemed that Nicole could have and would have, gone on in such a way she burst in to tears and cried on Marion's shoulder, deep, racking sobs that Emily and Sarah would have liked to have comforted, except that they felt so wrong and so ashamed of how they had behaved.

Marion was equally unimpressed. "If Emily did not have the good sense to tell her parents about what you two had planned, then at the very least *you* should have, young lady."

Sarah knew from experience that being called 'young lady', meant her mother was seeing her behaviour rather more as the 'young' than as the 'lady'. It was ironic, rather like a sarcastic school teacher calling a particularly naughty schoolboy, "-My fine young man," where "villain" might be more appropriate.

Crispin put his somewhat aristocratic nose in the air and announced:

"Our two families have discussed your punishment," he said severely. "We've decided that something rather drastic needs to be done to teach . . . ah . . . appropriate behaviour".

"Your horses will be removed for three months and put out to agistment. You will not leave the house without the express permission of your parents and you will have extra household duties. When you have shown yourselves worthy of our respect and trust again, these conditions will be lifted."

To the girls, shattered by their experiences of the past nearly eight hours, which had seemed a life-time of terror, the attitude of their parents, though understandable, was the last straw. They burst into paroxysms of tears and fled wailing into Emily's bedroom, locked the door and hugged each other for comfort, howling in despair.

Their parents moved uncomfortably around the lounge room. Discipline had been called for and they had delivered but it seemed that they had overdone it. They wished they had not mentioned punishment until at least the next day and after expressing appropriately their joy at the girls' safe return.

They had in fact hugged them and wept with them when they first saw them, when the police brought them back to the farm and told them the story, as they, the police, understood it to be from what they had been told. They had fed the hungry girls and had sent them off to shower and freshen up.

They should have realized what a highly fragile emotional state the girls would be in. From their point of view, Graham's reaction after hearing the girls were safe and relatively unharrmed, showed the mixture of each one's emotions.

He had said: "Thank God. Thank God," then added, "I'll kill them for putting us through this." These contradictions sumed up what they all felt: relief that the girls were safe and anger at their stupidity.

Eventually the mothers were able to gain access to Emily's room and hold their daughters and listen to the whole story—their silly idea, their terror and pain of capture and the threats against them, their escape and recapture, the ugliness of the boat trip, the agony of the bonds eating into their wrists, being thrown into the boot of the car and their fears that they may never see their families again. The fathers listened outside the door in a rather diminished state of anger.

Eventually Emily had said:

"It's not that you aren't right to punish us, Mum. We deserve it. We've been particularly, dangerously, silly and it was all my fault, my idea. We just hoped for a bit more comfort first. We were so unhappy and so looking forward to home that it . . . this was all a bit . . . much."

"We will hug you as long as you like," said Nicole and Marion quickly agreed. "I think we should stay with you all night and hold you while you sleep and recover. Anything nasty can wait for tomorrow."

"Or the next day," said Marion. "What you need now is to know only how worried we were because we love you so much. We only became cross that you put us through such agony."

"However, it is obvious that the greater agony, by a long way, was yours. For now you have been punished more than enough," added Nicole.

The two men waiting in the passage silently agreed. They moved back to the lounge to fortify themselves with, "A stiff drink." Perhaps, after all, there would be value in what had happened. The girls already seemed more mature in their attitudes.

Perhaps they should be as well.

PART 2

The Return of the Gang

Chapter One

Officer Hutchinson Regrets

Officer Hutchinson cursed under his breath for the fiftieth time. He had been on the edge of his greatest triumph and he had blown it. With his terrible mistake had gone not only his success but his promotion to sergeant. Who could say how long it would be before he had the chance of promotion again? He had been so angry with himself that he had offered to resign from the police force. At first, the station Superintendent had been inclined to accept it. It was just as well that Superintendent Walker had a lifetime of slow and deliberate action behind him. When he had thought about it for a bit he realised that it would be his loss as well as Hutchinson's: the officer was probably his best policeman. "Let him suffer for a while," said Walker to his wife. "Then we can be sure that he will never, *never* repeat that mistake."

It was amazing how little satisfaction you could get from cursing at a time like this, Hutchinson noticed. No amount of anger, no amount of swearing, no amount of self-blame, no amount of alcohol drunk could change anything that had happened. Quite simply it had happened and that was that. He knew he had to just get on with things; to put it all behind him and to get it right the next time.

But it did not help that his fiancée looked at him crossly with those big eyes that had so impressed him when he had first met her. It certainly did not help that his colleagues grinned at him when he went past and muttered, "Caution, Hutchie-!" He'd hit the next one that said it. He noticed that fewer of them were saying it today; they could tell that they were skating on thin ice and that he could easily punch their lights out in the near future. Maybe also they were beginning to feel sorry for him.

Yes, it was all because he had missed giving a simple cauion that he was in this mess, a mess that he had made entirely for himself. He had chased the fleeing criminals who had robbed the electronics store of so many expensive items: twenty-five $2,000 flat screen High Definition Digital TVs, fifty Blue Ray DVD players and seventy top-of-the-range lap-top PCs, averaging $1,200-plus each in value. He had caught the gang when they crashed while speeding through a red light.

He had also saved the two girls the thieves had kidnapped. These girls, Emily and Sarah, had seen the gang land on the beach near Elwood farm, recently bought by Emily's Dad. Foolishly they had followed them to their hiding place in the bush above the farm and had watched them burying the loot in strong plastic bags in a water-proof hiding place in the bush. The girls had been captured, threatened, tied up, and, after an escape attempt that failed, pushed in to a sail locker on the gang's yacht. Finally they had been thrown into the boot of their car. The girls had avoided gags by promising not to call out but when Officer Hutchinson and his partner had stopped the car and questioned the thieves, Emily had kicked on the boot lid and alerted him. After a scary chase the thieves had crashed the car—and Hutchinson had them.

That was when he made his mistake. He took the gang back to the police station and questioned them and the girls about their activities. He was so pleased with himself that he couldn't wait to charge the gang with breaking and entering, with theft of the goods, with kidnapping, with avoiding arrest—and even with speeding, running a red light and failing to wear seat belts.

He was so excited about his great success, in fact, that he had forgotten to caution them, the bit when you tell them that anything they say may be taken down and used as evidence against them. He had wondered why they had looked so pleased with themselves and why they had spoken so excitedly to the lawyer who was called in to represent them.

Then came the bombshell. The lawyer had insisted that his clients be released without charge because correct procedures had not been followed. If Hutchinson had not been so keen about charging the gang with everything he could think of that they could possibly have done, if he had only kept a few charges back, then he could have picked them up again outside, cautioned them after this and at least would have had something to charge them with.

The police were able to find the stolen goods, as the girls had told them where they were. The girls themselves were safe but the gang members: 'Shelly' Beach, 'Shady' Jenkins and 'One-Shot' Oakshott walked free, with the station superintendent looking so angry that Hutchinson was sure he would explode. With that anger went any chance of promotion. Hutchinson went from being on top of the world to wishing that the ground would open up and swallow him. He felt physically sick and had to go out to the back of the station and sit in a spare space in the car park with his head between his knees.

Almost worse was having to ring Emily and Sarah's parents the next morning to tell them what he had done. Graham, Emily's father, had gone quiet on the phone while Hutchinson blundered and stumbled through his explanation. He knew he was now going to seem to be a complete idiot for what he'd done and it was as if his body had said to him that he needed to sound like one as well. Finally Graham had said:

"I see, Officer Hutchinson. You have completely failed in your duty of care towards my daughter and her friend. You have allowed three dangerous criminals to walk free. What assurances can you give that the girls will be safe from these monsters who may seek to take revenge?"

"Oh, no, Mr Wood," stuttered Hutchinson. "I'm sure they wouldn't dare. It would just be too obvious . . . who they were and, uh, what they would be doing. They could never, uh, get away with it."

"One would have thought," said Graham icily, "That they would not have got away with larceny and kidnapping and assault of my daughter and her friend. So who knows what else they may believe they will get away with?"-

Officer Hutchinson had really no reply to this. What could he say? He had believed that what he had said would be obvious to anyone but he was no longer sure of anything. He was a decent man, was popular and would normally have been considered very capable. His error and its consequences had completely shaken his faith in himself and it would take time to restore his self-belief.

Little did he know that his reassurances to Graham would turn out to be as misguided as his cautioning error had been and as groundless.

Poor Officer Hutchinson; poor Graham; poor Emily and Sarah.

Chapter Two

The Gang Does Some Plotting

Shady Jenkins sipped his beer thoughtfully. Shady was a bit slow in his thinking and he would certainly not have known how to describe what he was doing. He was thinking back to what they had done and how it had all gone wrong. Only a miracle, Officer Hutchinson's failure to caution, had kept them out of jail. For the rest, the operation, the theft from the electronics store, their elaborate hideaway that no one could have known about had all gone horribly wrong.

"Curse them interferin' girls," he said finally.

He had said what the other two had been thinking. Shelly, the clever member of the gang, perhaps would have said it a little more eloquently but One-Shot would have put it exactly as Shady did. They were certainly pleased to have escaped jail but they had believed their little plan to have been fool-proof.

The hiding place for the stolen goods had been provided by One-Shot who had grown up on the farm, where his father had been the farm hand for a previous owner. Shelly had provided the organisation, the plan and the means for making the hiding place work. With their own van and car and a stolen yacht (thanks to the technical and automotive skills of Shady) the gang had been able to keep the stolen goods away from the suspcious eyes of the police, who could not charge them for the theft of goods they did not appear to have.

Now all their work had come to nothing and the expected profit had gone with it. In fact things had become so desperate that if they did not do something soon, they might even have to look for a job. This was not a situation that appealed to any of them and so they sat in a pub near Shelly's place, cursed the girls and scratched their heads purposefully, as if this would provide the answer.

"I'd sure like t' get back at them girls!" snarled One-Shot.

Shelly was being more practical and thinking how they might make some money but One-Shot's comment gave her an idea. She went quiet as she thought through how it might work. Eventually she said carefully,

"How would it be if we combined getting back at them with making some money?"

"Great!" said Shady and One-Shot at the same time.

"But how?" asked One-Shot.

"We kidnap them and hold them for ransom," said Shelly.

The two men gasped and One-Shot blasphemed. Shady looked at him disapprovingly. Most of his limited schooling had been with the Nuns when he had lived in the old run-down Olympic Village of West Heidelberg. Though he could steal without giving it a second thought, he prided himself that he was a good Catholic. He did not take the Lord's name in vain and he treated women with respect.

A nosy priest once wanted Shady to come to Confession and to attend church each Sunday. Shady's response was that he went to church "real regular", by which he meant, but felt he did not need to explain, once a year at Christmas time and once on Easter Sunday.

Mind you, this modest respect for his church did not lead Shady to avoid such "necessary" actions as kidnapping girls who had upset his plans for easy money. But he drew the line at what he called "funny business", which he found far from funny in a comic sense. These were harmful crimes against defenceless women and children and were the acts of "low life" as he put it.

One-Shot apologised for his language and Shady nodded. Then they turned and gave Shelly their full attention.

She was clever, they both thought. If Shelly thought kidnapping would work, there was a good chance that it would and they wanted to hear what she had in mind.

Shelly spelled out the details to a rapt and appreciative audience. Shady and One-Shot had been taking their breath in slowly and then holding it as they listened, in case even breathing might interrupt the wonder of Shelly's clever plan. Now that she had finished for the moment, they let it out suddenly and then drew in a swift and noisy breath of wonder. Shelly smiled. It was nice to be appreciated, even if these two were not the sharpest tools in the toolbox.

There were details to be worked out, such as where they would take the girls, where they could hide them and where the first ransom payment would be left. Shelly planned a dummy payment drop to frighten off the obvious police presence that would be waiting. How would she organise that and the second payent? Other details were needed but the main elements of the plot had been set in place.

They must sit down somewhere quiet and work out answers to these and a number of other questions that her plan raised. Still, it was "game on" and the thought made all three both excited and a little nervous at the same time.

Chapter Three

Sarah Stays with Her Friend

Graham Wood was not a happy man. He was so cross with Officer Hutchinson for the gang's escape that he seethed with anger and resentment. When the girls had been found and returned safe and more or less sound he had praised Officer Hutchinson for his quick action in chasing after and catching the three who had held his daughter, Emily, and her friend, Sarah as captives and who had treated them so roughly.

Now, however, Hutchinson had become in his mind the old-fashioned typical image of the stories and, because he was old enough, Agatha Christie's bumbling policeman. He thought of the police in Sherlock Holmes Poirot and Miss Marple. It was through Sherlock Holmes' brilliance and/or the cleverness of Poirot or Miss Marple that the crimes were solved. The police take the obvious (and misguided) course of action while the hero (or heroine) unravels all the clues and eventually show the police to have been completely wrong.

So would Emily and Sarah be safe? He certainly hoped so but in the near future he was going to keep his daughter on a short leash. He smiled to himself at the image of comparing her to a dog. Certainly she came when she was called, something that would have been far less obvious before her kidnap, but that was as far as it went. How closely could he control her to make sure she was safe? Control that was too strict would make her complain of being treated as a baby; too much freedom and neither he nor she would think she was safe.

One side effect of the girls' nightmare adventure was that they had become totally dependent on each other. After the drama had been sorted out—if you can sort out such trauma in any time other than years—Sarah's parents, Marion and Crispin, had packed the car to return to Melbourne, as they did after every weekend at the cottage on the farm. Sarah had then burst into floods of tears and begged to stay with Emily. Emily had begged Sarah's parents that she should stay also.

After much humming and hahing from both sets of parents, it was decided that Sarah would stay with the Woods on the farm for the time being. She could be enrolled at Emily's school at Belton for the rest of the term at least. This was about another five weeks. The school had already been in touch and the Principal had said that Emily should stay at home for as long as she needed. The School Counsellor had also rung and had spoken to Emily at length and had said that Emily could come and see her and talk about her ordeal if that would help.

Both sets of parents had been impressed by the kindness and consideration shown and this had played a part in Sarah being allowed to stay. Crispin would come down every Friday evening and Marion would stay on for a while to support Sarah further. Crispin had to return: he had already missed some days of work and there was too much piling up for him to put it off any longer.

So Sarah stayed. When they went to school the first time they were mobbed by curious students. They had become celebrities.

"Like was it, like bad?"

"Like, did ya cry?"

"Were ya hit? OMG. How much? Did it, like, hurt?"

"Did they . . . the guys, I mean . . . Like *do* anythin'?"

Emily and Sarah answered all their questions. In telling the story they became, in their own imaginations, pretty cool and brave. It was the only way to go, they said. The gang were, like, bad but they didn't do anything like they said, yeah. They only wanted their stolen electronics stuff and in making money from that stuff. They, Emily and Sarah, had stopped them getting away with it. Yeah, it wasn't cool that the police stuffed up and the gang got off. No, they weren't scared about that. The police would be, like, on to them.

Yes, Sarah was going to stay a while. She wanted to and, like they were best friends from way back.

"That's gay. You two goin' to get married, eh?" teased one boy. Everyone laughed and this was the only time the girls felt uncomfortable.

"What computers did they steal?" asked one girl whose life was lived around computers.

"No idea," said the girls together. "We weren't *that* close when they were burying stuff," said Sarah.

"We were hidin' 'cause we thought we'd watch and then, like, call the cops," said Emily.

"Why didn't ya get away?" asked the annoying boy. "Ya sneeze or cough or somethin'?"

"No," said Sarah. "The horses made the noise and they '-eard that."

"'orses eh?" he sneered. "That's gay. Ya're up yaselves"

He'd gone too far. These girls had been on TV and anyway, quite a few kids rode horses. This was the country and there was plenty of room for them. They rounded on the boy and attacked him, especially the girls, until he slunk off and looked for other kids he could attack. He was not a happy kid, his home life was a bad joke and so he teased others. He liked it best when he had them in tears

Chapter Four

The Kidnap

The girls would normally have caught the bus to school but Graham and Natalie were being very careful and they drove them each day for a period of time. After about a week of this the girls said they would be fine and that they would be walking to the bus together anyway, so they would feel quite safe.

It sounded reasonable, so the parents agreed.

What none of them knew was that they were being watched from some distance by One-Shot though powerful binoculars; stolen, of course. He had been quite patient. He had started watching towards the end of the week that Graham had been driving the girls to school. He was worried this might happen for many weeks and he was delighted when he saw that the girls had decided to walk to the bus after a week of being driven.

This would be their opportunity. The path to the bus left the farm and went straight for about one hundred metres to a gate before turning a corner where there were bushes forming a sort of hedge. After about another fifty metres; the path joined the road where the girls would catch the bus. There was a shelter at the bus stop. In the past there had been quite a few children from nearby farms who had caught the bus there but at the moment this stop served only Emily—and now Sarah.

One-Shot had caught the bus there himself as a child, although he had only gone to secondary school until fifteen, at which age, in those days, you could leave. Later he had realised that it would have been better if he had stayed on but no one could have told him that at the time. He was basically lazy and after he had tried a few jobs, he found that each employer expected too much of him for his liking. Especially, he was expected to do as he was told and he didn't like anyone bossing him around. He drifted into petty crime and of course was eventually caught.

At first it was just a warning, then juvenile detention and finally he had ended up in prison where he'd met Shady.

One-Shot knew from experience exactly where he and Shady could hide and wait for the girls, where they couldn't be seen until their victims had gone past and could be jumped and have a bag put over their heads. They would be out of sight of the farm and they could grab them before the bus arrived. They would have to gag them because other-wise they would scream and bring help.

The best idea would be to then wait in hiding until the bus gave up on the girls and went on to the next pick-up. Then they could get the girls to the car that they would have parked out of sight just around the corner. They would throw them on the back seat. Putting them in the boot would have treated them the same way as before. It would be a dead give-away, Shelly had said. Boy she was smart; she thought of everything.

When One-Shot reported back to Shelly and Shady, his partners in crime were impressed by what he had managed to sort out. It was Monday, the girls' first day of getting the bus to school. The parents would still be on the alert, so they decided to wait until Thursday.

Thursday is a sort of nothing day; it is not the start of the school and working week, it is not the middle of the week and it is not the end of it. Nothing much happens on Thursday. Even the TV is terrible, with repeats and, in the winter, football shows that might once have been funny. It was on a Nothing—Thursday that the gang had decided to strike.

They'd found a shed on a run-down farm: far enough away not to be an obvious place to search and near enough to be a fairly short trip.

The old farmer was past being effective and only left his house to milk his few cows out of habit. His main income was now the pension but he did not want to move in to town and be cooped up in a retirement village or Age Care hostel. The farm had been his life and he would die there.

The shed was sturdily built. The old farmer had once stored and repaired his farm machinery there, had stored feed for the hens he no longer had and had even, in his early years, churned his butter there. The shed had a number of rooms, large and small. It was well away from the house, not that that mattered as the old man was half blind and needed the hearing aids he refused to use. It suited them perfectly.

Thursday came around quickly. Shady and One-Shot had sneaked up to the bushes by the path outside the gate before it was light. They hid themselves and waited. They were a bit hung-over. They needed an alibi and Shelley had decided that the best way would be to have been drinking at the pub until it closed. They could then say that they had slept in that morning to sleep off the effect of their binge. How could they have been kidnapping girls when they were hung over and sleeping it off?

The trouble was that they had acted the part too well the night before and when Shelley came knocking at 4.30 am they had felt that they really did need a sleep in. Instead they were faced with a very early morning. They had staggered out of bed, cursing at what they had agreed to do. Shelley was insistent rather than sympathetic: this was the day for the kidnap; they would have to get on with it, no matter how they felt. In the hiding place, One-Shot was dying for a cigarette. He would normally have had six before the girls came down the path to the bus but he couldn't that morning. He had to make do with three he had smoked on the way. It was too dangerous to smoke there. The smoke might be seen at the house, especially if he set fire to the dry grass or some of the dead bits in the bushes. So he gritted his teeth and waited. It was a pleasant morning when Emily and Sarah set out.

The air was crisp but not cold. It was March, that best time of the year in Victoria, with generally cool mornings and evenings and delightfully warm days. Every now and then the day became almost too warm and you were reminded that summer had only just gone; and every now and then the day was really cool, to remind you that winter was just around the corner. That day was one of the perfect ones, although you might have had difficulty telling that to Shady and One-Shot. They'd been still in the bushes for more than three hours when the girls finally shut the farm gate and turned the corner and walked past them.

As they leapt from their hiding place, wearing their Super-Hero masks, they almost stumbled and fell flat on their faces, as their legs had gone stiff from being cramped up in the bushes. The girls wheeled around but their screams died in their throats as they were struck on the side of the head with hard fists, whirled around and quickly gagged with duct tape and a supermarket recyclable bag thrust over their heads. Then they were dragged back deep into the bushes and forced more or less face down in the grass. Realising what was happening—and guessing why—they started to struggle, until another swift blow to the head made them realise that resistance was useless.

In times of crisis our bodies work over-time. It's called the "fight or flight" reaction. Emily and Sarah could neither fight nor fly, their captors had seen to that. Instead they shivered almost uncontrollably, earning themselves another slap. At least their brains were working; in fact they were working over-time. Their brains told them that their best hope was that they were able to stay conscious and be able to react to, or at least remember, what happened to them and how long they would travel. They had already worked out that it was Shady and One-Shot; despite the disguise; who had captured them. What these two could not disguise was their size and the way they moved. The girls had caught a glimpse of the two in their masks just as they were being grabbed.

They said nothing, however, as they were worried what the two would do if they knew that they had been recognised. Shady and One-

Shot had gone to great trouble over their disguises. The girls, who knew how their captors reacted when things were going against them, were afraid that they would be very angry to have been exposed. They would become more violent than they had been so far.

Emily was worried also about how she would be able to breathe. When the gang captured them on the hill, she had begged to be able to avoid a gag. Now she was gagged, she struggled to breathe. Normally well-mannered and elegant, Emily became a sniffling, snuffling mess gagged. as she desperately tried to clear at least one nasal passage to allow air through.

Shady was very tempted to tell her she was disgusting but didn't want his voice to be recognised. Fortunately for Emily, although she gurgled through her nose, she was at least able to get adequate air. She remembered her father saying that mostly whatever you want enough in life you will be able to get. Emily really wanted to breathe; she really wanted to stay alive.

Shady and One-shot waited until the school bus arrived. They could glimpse the bus driver scratching his head and watching through the bus window for the girls to appear. Normally, if they were not coming to school, he would have had a phone call to let him know. No such call had been made but the girls were not there. Maybe they were not well. Maybe the ordeal they had been through was catching up on them. He waited a while and then drove off, to the satisfaction of the two kidnappers and to the horror of the girls. When the coast was clear the kidnappers crawled out of the hiding place. One-Shot watched the girls and Shady ran around the corner to where he had hidden the car. To vary the kidnap routine from after the boat trip, One-Shot and Shady threw the girls on to the back seat rather than in the boot. Then they threw themselves in to the car and drove off at quite a fair speed. One-Shot heard another car door slam and realised that Emily's father or mother must have waited until they heard the bus leave the gate before going out to the shops. In fact it was Emily's mother who was going out. She had a hair appointment in the town at 9.30 am. While it would take her only ten to fifteen minutes to get there, Natalie liked to be early. She would browse in the second-hand bookshop that, surprisingly, opened at 8.30 a.m. After about 20 minutes or so she would perhaps buy a book or two before a quiet stroll along the main street to be well on time for the appointment.

Natalie would not have been so relaxed if she had known what was actually going on that morning. As she hummed happily to herself, her daughter and her friend's daughter were trussed up like Christmas turkeys on their way to the processing plant. Unlike the turkeys, the girls were well aware that this trip could be their last. They knew that could easily be killed if things did not go the kidnappers' way.

Chapter Five

The Hiding Place

About twenty minutes after they set off, Shady and One-Shot arrived at the small gravel road that provided access to the back of the old man's farm. If there had been any doubt before about the identity of their kidnappers, by the time they got there the girls were sure. One-Shot had a distinctive and slightly high-pitched cough that came from too many cigarettes over too many years. Shady did not approve of his habit and would utter a disapproving "harrruuumph", a sort of growl from the back of his throat, whenever One-Shot lit up. Both the cough and the grunt were familiar to the girls from their previous adventure and they almost giggled out loud, despite their discomfort, when they heard them.

The room where the gang members would keep the girls had been well-prepared by Shelly. There were a couple of air beds on the floor and there was a portable toilet in one corner. The room had been chosen because it had a wash basin on the back wall that had once been used to clean the butter churn. Shady had fixed concrete-reinforcing steel mesh (what builders call 'Reo') to the outside of the small window that was the only access to the world beyond the room. As an extra precaution against both escape and the possibility of being heard, the window had been nailed shut.

Food was also provided, so that the kidnappers would not have to go in and be seen. There was fresh drinking water available in the form of three ten-litre casks of 'Spring' water, such as you can buy from a Supermarket. This was in case the tap water proved to be undrinkable through the build-up of rust in the pipes. That water would nevertheless be useful for washing—and four small towels had been provided for this, plus some liquid soap.

The sliced bread they found would be fresh for only a couple of days, after which they would have to eat rye crisp-bread or rice cakes. The small bar fridge with an extension lead through to the machinery room contained butter and long-life milk, packets of vacuum-sealed meat slices, jam and peanut butter. There were a few tins of sardines and tuna snacks on the table. The girls were not going to starve for at least a week, if they ate sensibly.

The entrance to the girls' room was through another room, the machinery room. Here stood an ancient Ferguson tractor that had not been started up in years but had been kept by the old farmer, partly as a reminder that he had once been a farmer, partly because he insisted that it might still be useful and partly because he had been told that its only value would be as scrap. Shady and One-Shot had set this area up as their room.

It had the bare necessities, as they would come and go. They could eat take-away at the small table but they would shower elsewhere. In fact it was their intention that they would mostly be elsewhere, at their normal pub, for instance, where they could be seen as not being the kidnappers of the girls.

Once they had been thrown in to their room, the girls' hands had been freed and while they were removing their gags and their blindfold bags, Shady and One-Shot had slammed the door and were out of sight. They stood back and held their breath, then smiled, as the girls alternately screamed and pleaded with them to be released. This was to be expected and it gave them the opportunity to go out of the shed complex and listen to what could be heard.

They were pleased to hear that only muffled sounds found their way outside. The old farmer, some distance away and hard of hearing, watching television, pottering about making meals and sleeping well away from the sheds, should be no problem.

Shady and One-Shot gave each other the thumbs up sign then, really pleased with themselves at the success of the morning's work, gave each other high fives. The girls would be safely locked up where they were, the prison in which they found themselves was well chosen and secure.

They could relax and leave them. The girls would soon get tired of screaming and shouting. When no one came to rescue them they would settle down, exhausted by their efforts and by energy spent on anxiety and they would then be considerably quieter.

Chapter Six

The Pub Alibi

It was time to report back to Shelly and, very importantly, it was time to be seen at the pub. They would sneak in the back way and join Shelly at a little table in the corner of the lounge. It was out of sight of the bar.

Shelly had ordered them a beer each which she had then taken to her imaginary companions in the lounge. Most of contents of these beers had been carefully poured into pot-plants. When the barman came around to collect glasses, Shelly had told him that they were in the toilet. Apart from an actual sighting of Shady and One-Shot, it would seem to the barman that they had been there for some time before they actually arrived. Shelly smiled at her cunning. The police would have some trouble charging them for a kidnap at which they could not have been present.

Shady and One-Shot got back to the pub in very smart time, especially considering that, once in the city, Shady had insisted on using back streets to avoid being seen by anyone who might recognise them. As soon as they were in the back door of the hotel and safely in the lounge, they quickly drank what was left of the beer and began to quarrel. The barman came to see what the matter was.

"What's the problem, guys?" said the barman.

"One-Shot says he paid for the last beer," said Shady, pretending to be angry. "But he didn't. I did."

"You're both wrong," said Shelly. "I paid for them, didn't I, Steve?"

Steve the barman nodded. "Cool it, fellers," he said. "-One of you two can buy the next round and the other one the round after that."

"OK", said Shelly when the barman had gone back to work. "Things is goin' well. We've made the snatch and you're here and 'ave been seen. We've 'idden '-'em somewhere we can leave 'em. Bein' here throws the police off the scent. In fact this is the perfect pub for our plan. Willie Williams, who's just come in, is a police snitch an' he drinks 'ere all the time. Don't look now but he's spotted us and he's comin' over. He'll tell 'em we was here and us sayin' as 'ow we wished it was us that took 'em."

"Hello, Shelly, hello boys", said Willie. "Been busy today, have you?"

"What d'ya mean?" snarled Shady. "What d'ya think ya can pin on us now? What are we supposed t'ave done?"

"Don't play th' innocent with me. Those girls ya took a while back. Just heard on the car radio. They've been took again earlier t'day."

"Well, it'd be real smart fer us to've done it, wouldn't it?" asked Shelly. "S'-pose this means the cops'll be crawlin' in all over us any minute now. Lucky fer us, we been 'ere."

"Yeh, but fer 'ow long?" sneered Willie. "They was taken at about 8.30. Ya'd 'ave 'ad enough time ta stash 'em and get back here by now."

"Not that it's any ya business", snarled Shelly, "But we've been 'ere since the place opened at ten. I s'pose they was at school at Belton when they was taken. How we s'posed t'ave taken 'em down there at 8.30, stashed 'em somewhere, which'd 've took time, an' got back 'ere fer ten o'clock openin'?"

Willie was thinking hard. Yes, it would have been tight, to say the least. Although Belton was only one and a half hours away itself, they'd have needed time to drop the girls somewhere, so they couldn't really have got back in time, not if they'd been here at opening time. The gang watched as his mind rolled on awkwardly It was as laboured as the old farmer's rusty tractor would have been if they'd tried to start it.

There was a long sigh, as Willie tried to figure it out, failed and went back to his usual drinking group. All the talk in the pub was about the disappearance of the girls. Out of the corner of their eyes, the gang members could see the furtive glances and half-hidden finger pointing as patrons who did not know the gang, or details of the previous kidnap, were brought up to speed on the story, considerably embellished and exaggerated. The notorious celebrities were pointed out. At one stage it became so obvious what was going on that Shelly decided it could not be ignored any longer.

"What are yous starin' at?" she shouted at one group. "-Mind ya own *^$#* business!"

"Keep ya shirt on, Shelly!" one called back. If ya goin-'to be famous, ya gotta expect people t'be innerested."

"I gotta better idea," said a newcomer, who was a smart-aleck, after checking Shelly out. "Take ya shirt *off*, Shelly!" There was loud laughter until Shady got to his feet and moved threateningly in his direction.

"Ya better get outa here!" warned one of the regulars. "-Nobody takes on Shady, not even in the toughest prison."

The newcomer, who had been prepared to be tough himself, suddenly decided to change his position and bolted out the door, while the regulars roared with laughter. Shady gave a grim smile and went back to his seat.

Chapter Seven

Hutchinson is Frustrated

Then Officer Hutchinson burst in to the pub, white-faced and stressed. He'd been yelled at by the Superintendent at his Police Station and threatened by a furious and desperate Graham Wood who had told him in no uncertain terms that he'd pay if the girls came to any harm—and what was he going to do about it? Hutchinson had no idea what he could do about it—but he felt both guilty and worried. It may not have been the gang who had the girls; in fact he really hoped wildly that it wasn't. However, the greatest likelihood was that it was in fact them. He knew where they drank in Port Melbourne and he hurried to check up on them.

Hutchinson went to the barman and asked him. "Yeah," said the barman. "I wondered that meself when I heard the story. But Shelly, Shady and One-Shot have been here all mornin'." They'll be well away by mid-afternoon at this rate. Don't see how they could've done it and got here by ten."

Now, as we know, they hadn't been there by 10.00 a.m. but Shelly's trick had worked. The barman believed that they must have been there because, through Shelly, "they" had ordered drinks. Why, they'd even quarrelled about whose round it was!

Hutchinson scratched his head. It *had* to have been them! How had they managed it? If they were there, he wanted a word with them. He found out where they were sitting and stormed up to them.

"All right, you three. Where are they? What've you done with them?"

The gang pretended to be both shocked and insulted.

"Wha' d'ya mean Officer Hutchinson?" said One-Shot loudly, in indignant pretend surprise.

"I s'pose ya talkin' about the story I hear that them girls 'ave been snatched," said Shelly with a pained and serious look on her face. "And, of course, ya want t'blame us for it! Well, as ya can see it weren't us"

"Not much," said Hutchinson, "You three have the three elements needed for a crime like this: motive, means and opportunity".

"Wha'?" said One-Shot with his mouth open. "Ya lost me-".

"Wouldn't be hard", thought Hutchinson to himself. "He's not the sharpest knife in the drawer!" But he didn't say this, as he might need some cooperation, at least if he was going to find the girls alive.

"I mean," said Hutchinson, with more patience and self-control than he fet. "The 'motive' is wanting revenge for the warehouse theft cock-up. Not to mention being greedy for easy money. The 'means' is that you would know how to carry out such a crime. Ya've got access to vehicles t'get them to wherever ya've got them hid. I mean 'hidden'," he corrected himself as he noticed that he was starting to talk like the gang. And 'opportunity' because . . ." He paused to consider how he would put this. "Because none of you would have to take time off work to do it and because you know where Emily lives and you'll know that Sarah is staying with her at the moment."

"No, Officer Hutchinson, I didn't know that," said Shelly reasonably. "How would we? We're not exactly best mates with their parents."

Hutchinson felt frustrated. "You'd know", he said, hopefully. And when Shelly smiled a 'prove it' smile, he burst out: "You've probably been spying on them-!"

"You're losing it, Hutchinson," said Shelly in a superior voice. "Are you suggesting that we went spying on girls we didn't know were still together and somehow captured them while we were here, or, at the very least, at a time when we'd have needed a space ship to get back to this pub by opening time from the time we kidnapped them?"

"Just pop out the back, Officer, "said One-Shot getting in on the act. "Shady will give ya a lift in our spaceship."

"I'll take ya," said Shady, "But I won't bring ya back".

"We've hidden the girls on Mars," said Shelly helpfully. "Shady will show you where." The three crooks laughed loudly and gave each other high fives.

Hutchinson breathed a deep frustrated breath. He knew the gang must have been responsible but how could it be proved? He took his hat off and scratched his head".

"Keep scratchin', Hutchie," said One-Shot, thinking himself a great comedian. "Ya'll maybe find some part of a brain in there one day."

Chapter Eight

Plotting the Ransom

Hutchinson was forced to leave in a highly embarrassed state, with the gang laughing loudly, One-Shot at his own joke; the other two more from enjoyment at the policeman's embarrassment. They congratulated themselves at the success of Shelly's plan.

Shady stopped laughing quite suddenly.

"So far so good," he said, "But how're we goin' to collect the ransom? And how much ransom should we ask fer?"

Shelly looked thoughtful. "I been given' that my attention," she said.

She paused and the two men, nodding and smiling happily, waited for her to resume, knowing that she would in her own good time and knowing also that it was best not to interrupt her train of thought when she was planning something.

"The ransom note is simple," she said finally. "We use a computer. I kept one from the job, hidden at my place and a printer as well. We keep it simple and we print on the cheapest, most common paper. The amount? There's two families. I reckon they're not poor and anyway, if we wait for a bit, they'll be desperate and pay whatever we ask. On the other hand, we don't want to appear too greedy; not fer starters, any'ow."

They wanted to ask questions about this but Shelly held up her hand in objection and they stayed quiet.

"What's tricky is collectin' the ransom money without bein' seen. The police is sure t' be there. What I think I'll do is give Willie Williams an anonymous tip off about where the drop will be. He's a greedy bastard an' he won't be able t' resist. '-E'll go just a bit earlier than the note says and, of course the families will 'ave the money there ahead of the time.

We'll watch 'im and when th' police nab 'im we'll send another note warnin' the parents that if they 'ave the police at the next drop, the girls will die. We'll 'ave no trouble a second time."

"One 'a the good things about this is the fun we'll 'ave 'earin' about 'ow Willie explains 'is attempt ta pick up the ransom."

Shady and One-Shot were grinning. They liked it.

"We'll ask fer three quarters of a million," said Shelly. "I ackchuly want one million, so we get over three hundred each. We ask fer that the second time. It's a penalty increase fer 'avin' the police fer the first drop."

The two men grinned again. It just got better and better.

"Now fer the ransom note," said Shelly.

Chapter Nine

The Girls' Prison

Once they knew that Shady and One-Shot had gone and that they could not make anyone hear, the girls' mood turned to despair.

"How long will they keep us here?" wondered Sarah.

"At least until our parents pay a ransom demand," said Emily and added, "-But what if they ask for too much? What if or parents can't afford to pay? What if . . ."

"What if the gang get the ransom and then decide to kill us anyway? They might think that freeing us is too much of a risk." added Sarah, echoing what they both were thinking.

They shuddered. They suddenly felt very vulnerable.

"Whatever we do, we mustn't let them know that we know who they are!" said Emily forcefully. "That *would* be a death wish."

Sarah didn't need any convincing. They were in danger, a genuinely scary feeling of danger. It was exactly what they had felt when the gang had first captured them on the hill at Emily's parents' farm. They had survived then but would they survive again? Both had a sneaking suspicion that they could not be that lucky twice.

They stood shivering.

Eventually Emily said, "Well, we won't get anywhere just standing here feeling sorry for ourselves. Let's at least look around and see if there's any way out of here."

"There won't be," said Sarah miserably. "They're hardly likely to have left us nice girl-sized holes to squeeze through."

"Look, Sarah, you could be right but we can't be defeated before we start," said Emily. "We'd look pretty stupid if there *was* some way out and we hadn't even bothered to look for it."

They searched the room carefully. Although the walls were timber, the gang had been busy nailing up any loose boards and putting in extra nails here and there to make sure that there weren't any obvious weak points. They'd done this to the floor as well, covering one hole area with new pine boards. As has been explained, the windows were barred and nailed shut.

Perhaps the roof would be the best bet. Shed rooves are not lined and there is no ceiling between the pitch of the roof and the main part of the room. But this was an old shed, built in the days when rooms had more height than they do these days. This was in fact practical in an Australian summer. Heat rises and you don't want to be working inside on a hot day in February with heat trapped down low under corrugated iron.

The girls looked up in despair. Yes, if they could get up high they might have some chance of kicking off a sheet of corrugated iron and climbing out—but how were they going to get that high up? Standing on the table didn't get you high enough and it wouldn't have, unless they had been unusually tall, like an international basketball player. They sighed miserably.

The weakest point was possibly the door. The hinges didn't look all that strong. What would happen if they both rushed it with their shoulders at the same time?

"Probably break our shoulders," said Sarah pessimistically.

"Hang on," said Emily. "We've each been given a knife for spreading and cutting food up. They're only cutlery knives and not at all sharp but at least they're metal and not plastic. Perhaps we can scratch away at the hinges and see if we can work the screws out a bit—at least enough to weaken them even further."

"Great idea," said Sarah excitedly. "Even if they were only half out, or less even, we might be able to do the rest with our shoulders together. At least the door opens out to the other room, so pushing weaker screws really should work!"

Excitedly the girls rushed to the table where the knives were. They may have been metal, but they were not Sheffield's best, nor strong Scandinavian stainless steel. They were 'Target's, or maybe 'Big W's', made in some country with no history of quality cutleery. If they weren't careful, they'd just snap while they were working on the screws. They looked at each other with a mixture of hope and fear in their faces.

"We've got to try," said Emily with determination. "If we don't, we may never get out! We'll just have to take our time and not put too much force on the hinge at any one time. First, to get at the hinge properly, we have to push the piece of wood on this side of the hinge, whatever it's called."

"Is it the door jamb? asked Sarah.

"I don't know," said Emily. But if it is jammed in too hard, we really will be in a jam!"

"Or a pickle," laughed Sarah.

It was the first light moment they'd had since the capture and they giggled for some time, rather longer than the silly joke warranted—but they were letting out tension and they needed that.

"Come on," said Emily at last. "If we don't get started, we'll never do it. And we've got to get it done before One-Shot and Shady come back. I doubt they'll come too often and that's why we've got all that food. But you never know."

The girls started to work, carefully but with some urgency.

Chapter Ten

The Ransom Demand

Shelly composed the ransom note carefully. It needed to be as brief as would cover their need, but with enough detail so that it was clear what they wanted and where the drop would be. She had decided on the old trick of a drop in a rubbish bin, somewhere a motor bike could come past and snatch it and tear off at speed. She'd seen this in detective stories and films. Somewhere not too far away would be a lane, a mere gap between buildings that a bike could get through but a police car couldn't. Escape could appear to be made through this to a waiting car.

In fact, thought Shelly, surely the police would have seen these programs as well and would make allowance for the lane, stationing another police car the other end of it—a nasty surprise for Willie Williams.

Shelly wanted this plan therefore to appear fool-proof but not to be so. Willie would need to think it was good enough for him to get away with—but it should not be not so good that the police couldn't catch him. It was, in fact, most important that they did catch him so that Shelly could write a second, and more threatening, note to the girls' parents.

The ransom note she wrote was pretty standard, except for the spelling.

Weve got two girls with us. They tell us there names are Emily and Sara.

We will kill them if you dont meet our demands.

We want $750,000 in used notes in a plane brown bag left in a rubbish bin in Walker St, St Kilda just along from Mackas on the same side.

Leave it round 12.30 Satday nite.

No police

The kidnapers

Shelly got Shady and One-Shot to check it out and they couldn't see anything wrong with it—but then they were not giants in the English language and neither of them had gone further in school than Year Nine. They called it 'Sub-Intermediate', which it used to be in the old days. In fact neither of them even finished that year; school was never a favourite place for either of them.

"Looks good ta me," said One-Shot.

"Yeah, great," said Shady.

Shelly sighed. Fat lot of use they were when it came to something like that. "Might as well show it to that mongrel that's liftin' its leg on that rubbish bin", she thought, but she didn't say anything. "No point in getting them offside", she thought. She needed them and they were good at other things—like motors and anything needing muscle.

Shelly ran off two copies of this, one slightly different from the other. This second one she screwed up. It looked as if it had been rejected because of its spelling and other mistakes. She dropped this one in the hotel car park near Willie's car. When Willie was caught, he would say that he'd found the note there but how could he prove it? Shelly would simply say that of course Willie would try to pin the kidnap and ransom on them. She would pretend to be angry that the police believed him. It was harassment, she would say.

One-Shot hid in the car park shrubbery and watched to make sure that Willie found the note. They knew that he was a sticky-beak and Shelly had read him correctly. When he got near to his car, with his car keys in his hand, Willie saw the crumpled sheet of paper, bent down and picked it up. When he'd read what was on it, his eyes bulged in his head. He looked quickly around him to see if anyone had seen him read it.

One-Shot held his breath and crouched motionless in the shrubbery. Willie had licked his lips in anticipation of the three quarters of a million dollars he expected to get out of his amazing good fortune. One-Shot could hardly contain himself. He almost gave the game away and had to control the huge laugh, really more a high-pitched giggle, that bubbled up inside him. He swallowed hard to avoid this and forced himself to stay still. He imagined himself stalking a deer in the bush, as he had when young.

One time with his father he had become really excited. He had moved and cried out when a deer appeared. The deer disappeared into the bush in a flash. His father had been really angry, as he knew that all game in the area would have gone far away out of reach as a result. One-Shot had been belted across the head and the ears for this. He couldn't move then for some time as he wanted to vomit every time he did and he was still somewhat deaf in that ear.

Now he almost groaned as he remembered it and he had to stifle that as well. Fortunately for him, Willie neither saw nor heard him. He was too excited by what he'd found. He was already planning his next move as he got into his car and drove out of the car park. This was going to be too easy. The parents, he worked out, wouldn't risk involving the police and they would drop the money well before the deadline to be safe. He'd get there before the gang. All he had to do was to plan an escape route from the drop site. The girls would be in danger from the gang when they found no money in the bin—but that was not his problem. If they came to harm it would be the gang

Who would be blamed? Not him. He was blinded by the expectation of three quarters of a million dollars. So much! And he didn't need to split it with anyone!

Willie was so excited he nearly side-swiped an old lady with dyed hair who was driving what had probably been her dead husband's Toyota. She was crawling along the street after her supermarket shopping, believing that by driving slowly she was driving safely, avoiding speed.

Willie had to brake late and hard to avoid her. His muttered curses were too rude and nasty to be recorded, even though the situation was caused largely by his own lack of concentration. It's difficult to concentrate after the sudden expectation of three quarters of a million dollars and to focus on what a little old lady is doing in a car in which she had been mainly a passenger for fifteen years.

Meanwhile, One-Shot was hurrying back into the pub to report the success of the scheme to Shelly and Shady. He'd waited in the shrubbery for a few minutes, just to make sure that Willie had not become suspicious and done a U-turn in the street nearby so he could return to check. In fact Willy was so wrapped up in his dream of a $750,000 dollars, that, as we have seen, he was having enough trouble driving safely in a straight line. He had no room in his greedy brain for checking the reality of the note by fancy driving that might lead him to discover the reason for its being there.

What is more, Willie, who could spell better than the gang members, assumed that this note had been thrown out, admittedly rather carelessly, because it was a first draft. Shelly had wanted this to look like a first attempt by deliberately adding some errors to the note Willie had found. For example, this note had a jump to a new line half way through a sentence. It read:

We will kill them if you don't mete our demands.

and other mistakes:

$750,000 in new noats ina plane brown bag.

She tried not to overdo the mistakes, however. It would cause Willie to be suspicious if it was too obvious. In fact she didn't know how many mistakes the note contained, as she didn't know how many spelling errors there were. It was more obviously fake than she knew but Willie's greed convinced him that it was really a draft. The "draft" did include, of course, where the drop was to be and when. There was not much point in Willie knowing there was a ransom demand if he didn't know that.

The scene had been set for the ransom demand to be delivered. It would have to be posted to the parents, as dropping it off by hand was too risky. Shelly decided that a postmark from Port Melbourne would also cause suspicion to fall on them.

She took the envelope and the note, both of which she'd handled only with gloved hands, to the Toorak Post Office. The gang enjoyed her joke and her cleverness. A badly spelled ransom-note coming from Melbourne's wealthiest suburb appealed to them, even though they didn't know how badly spelled it was.

Everything was ready for the first stage of the ransom demand. Shelly would make sure that it went well by setting Shady and One-Shot in a car outside Willie's place. If he did get away with snatching the bag of money then that also suited them well. They would have the ransom to divide up once they'd got it from Willie, who'd have to give it up once Shady got his hands on him. Shady could be very persuasive.

Willie could hardly complain to the police about their "theft" when he'd been the one who'd grabbed the money from the bin. Even if the police believed him, how would he be able to explain why he hadn't reported his find to them in the first place?

If the police arrested Willie near the bin (the most likely outcome) the money would be returned to the parents who would quickly get the second ransom note with its heavier threat about polilce involvement.

Shelly then decided that it was time for the boys to go back to the farm and check on the girls.

Chapter Eleven

The Escape Attempt

Sarah inserted the knife in a small gap in the door jamb and tried carefully to prise out the nails that held it in. They held their breath in horror as the nearest nail moved only a very little while the knife bent alarmingly.

"We'll never do it," said Sarah with just a little hysteria in her voice.

"Wait on," said Emily, "The nail did move a little."

They stood still for a while, their bodies tense with worry.

"Perhaps we should use both knives together," said Sarah eventually. "If we held them with the same hand and pushed out carefully, that might work."

"Brilliant, Sarah," gasped Emily. "Great. Let's try it. It's your idea; you do it and I'll support and tell you how it's going."

"OMG," said Sarah, automatically dropping into school language. But she took the knives and put them in the gap, one each side of the nail that had moved a little.

To their surprise and delight, the nail moved quite easily with the extra pressure and the ones on each side came out enough for the same technique to free them up as well. In no time the old piece of wood was free and the hinges were exposed.

"Use the same idea on the hinges, Sarah," said Emily excitedly, staring at them up close. "I think they'll come out just as easily."

She was right and, with a crash the door fell out after the first push, hanging crazily on the other side from the padlock their captors had attached. They simply hadn't dreamed that the door would be opened from the other side.

Desperate people find desperate remedies.

The girls grabbed their belongings and a few biscuits and ran out of the building, across the yard where the cows had waited to be milked, over the fence and across the paddock towards where they expected the road to be.

For a while they got it slightly wrong, having taken their bearings from where the farm track ran out to the service road that in turn ended up at the main road.

Then, suddenly, they were on the main road and running towards where they hoped the nearest town was. They were starting to slow down now, gasping a bit more for air. A car coming along the road would be all they would need to gain a lift. The car, or at least the people in it, would probably have a phone. They could call their parents and then the police and tell them they were safe and free. Home, their parents, a hot bath, these were surely only about an hour away.

At last they saw a car in the distance and they waved at it as it came nearer. Then they saw it stop for a moment. Were the people in it wondering who these crazy girls were and discussing whether they should in fact stop at all? People these days are nervous about picking strangers up on the road. Even girls are suspect, as they may be simply the bait to make a car stop, so that hidden males could jump out of hiding places beside the road and rob and even kill the people who were being kind.

The girls discussed this possibility and decided the best thing would be to walk towards the car so that the people in it would not fear hidden attackers. As they did so, they decided that they must have been right, as the car started again towards them.

When it drew alongside, they were horrified to see two men in balaclavas and large sunglasses. The car had stopped so that the driver and passenger could pull these out from wherever they were kept and put them on.

Despite the disguise, which would have been laughable if it had not had such a sinister side to it, the girls immediately knew that, of all the cars that might have come along this road, this was the only one they did not want to see. It was the one they dreaded to see and, given the amount of food that they had been left, it was not one they had even remotely expected to see.

They knew immediately that they had fallen again into the nasty hands of Shady and One-Shot. Trying to run would have been futile. They were tired from their efforts to get free and their flight across the paddocks and along the road.

They groaned inwardly at their bad luck, which was more than doubly bad luck. If they had worked out their plan of escape earlier then they would have been much further up the road by now. Indeed they would no doubt have seen a different car and would have been on their way to safety instead of recapture.

Had they gone the other way along the road, Shady and One-Shot would have had to go the extra kilometres to the farm, where they needed to park their car by the side of the road and sneak across the paddocks to the shed, as they could not risk being seen by the old farmer. Half blind he might have been but he was not entirely so and he must not know what was going on. This would have given the girls at least another half an hour.

Had the girls actually gone up to the farmhouse, instead of trying to escape by running across the paddocks, they could have used the farmer's phone to ring for help. Why hadn't they thought of that? They knew the answer. They were so anxious to get away from their prison that they hadn't even considered it for a moment.

"Hello, girls," said the two voices they least wanted to hear.

"Going somewhere?" said the badly-disguised One-Shot.

Chapter Twelve

Willie's Dreams Become a Nightmare

Willie Williams could hardly wait for Saturday night. He slept badly the night before, but he had carefully checked out the drop-off zone. He decided that the best way to get away was a very narrow lane nearby that a police car would have trouble getting through and he had borrowed a motorbike from someone he knew, paying a generous amount for the privilege. With this he could snatch the ransom money and drive quickly to the lane. If there were any police on hand, he would be away before they could catch him.

The gang would be furious. They would have done all the kidnap work and he, Willie, would get all the money. He chuckled to himself. How lucky was he to have got his hands on a draft of the ransom note that Shelly, probably, had dropped accidentally? It couldn't have been deliberate, he thought, because why would they give up three quarters of a million dollars so easily?

. . . .

Graham looked at the ransom note in despair. Three quarters of a million dollars! It would take nearly all the money he had set aside in his Superannuation fund. Well, no, it wouldn't really because Crispin and Marion would have to pay half. And, despite the note, he was going to tell the police. They would arrange themselves very discreetly in the vicinity of the "drop" and catch the gang member who picked up the money. They would then force the gang to release the girls, perhaps with the promise of some reduction in their prison sentence if they cooperated.

Graham ground his teeth in frustration. What if the gang had, in fact, already killed the girls and they could not be rescued at all? What if the gang took the money, got away with it and then killed the girls so they couldn't tell the police who had taken them? This was a horribly likely scenario.

Damn that Hutchinson idiot who had failed to charge the gang properly! It was all his fault that this had happened!

He had rung Crispin. He in turn had been angry that he had allowed Sarah to stay at Ellwood Farm. If she had been at home, she'd have been safe in Melbourne. The gang would have been unable to snatch her there.

What a fool he'd been! He should have known, when the gang had escaped gaol on a technicality, that they would be looking for money and revenge at the same time. He also blamed Graham and Natalie for not supervising the girls properly. It wasn't the point that the girls had insisted that they would be all right. Adults had to make such decisions.

His anger and coldness had upset Graham, who needed comfort rather than criticism. He decided that Crispin, such a close friend for so long, wasn't really a friend at all! In this way, as in others, the kidnap could change their lives, perhaps for ever? However, he later realized that Crispin was speaking out of general fear and frustration and that he wouldn't continue to blame Graham.

Crispin's banks had to be told what was going on. No bank has $750,000 dollars just lying around in used notes to hand out at a moment's notice to meet the needs of a ransom demand. In fact this was the first time in Australian history that such a large amount had been demanded. It was just as well the two men used different banks.

It may not have been possible for one bank to have put such a large amount together in such a short time.

Eventually, however, the money was gained and put together in large paper bags, all placed in a strong orange garden bag so that there would be less reason for suspicion on the part of anyone who saw a bag being put into a rubbish bin. An ordinary black kitchen garbage bag would not have been strong enough. As the police pointed out, it would have been rather hard to explain a garbage bag flying apart after the kidnappers had snatched it, with large denomination bank notes flying around in the air and on the ground. While people passing by would be delighted, the kidnappers would have been very angry and would undoubtedly have harmed, if not killed, the girls.

At last all was prepared. Graham would make the drop about twenty minutes before the time mentioned, to allow the kidnappers time to see that the coast was clear and that they could safely come out (probably only one of them would) and snatch the money from the bin.

....

Willie waited in a dark lane on the motor bike he'd just borrowed. It was a trail bike, slim, strongly-sprung, but powerful, designed to dash along bush tracks in hilly country. It should be perfect for making the snatch, tearing off and bouncing along the blue-stone-paved lane to the road where, he imagined, the police would be unable to follow.

He grinned to himself. He was about to be rich and he would hide out in the country the next morning after ditching the bike a few streets away and changing to a car he'd "borrowed" a little earlier in the evening from outside a block of flats where it would not be missed until morning. He'd drive this to a town called Bacchus Marsh on the road to Ballarat, leave the car and catch the early train to Ballarat, where he could "borrow" another car.

However once there he'd play it by ear. Quite probably he'd simply catch the train back to Melbourne and stay in a motel until the coast was clear. He thought he should be able to afford a good motel and have his meals brought to him. He could afford a great deal more than this but he mustn't be greedy; it would give the game away.

Willie had a canvas bag on a belt around his shoulders. In the car he'd left a large suitcase with some change of clothing and sufficient room for the money as well. It would look less suspicious on the train than the canvas bag and, anyway, the police would no doubt use a description of the bag in the alert they'd put out in their attempt to find him. With the bike helmet, goggles and leathers (all to be left behind) they wouldn't have much of a description.

He was feeling very pleased with himself but couldn't help feeling a little nervous at the same time. What if he didn't time his approach to the bin properly? If he was too early, there wouldn't have been the drop; if he was too late the gang would have the money before he got there.

He looked at his watch. Midnight. He'd go at 12.15 a.m. That should allow him the best chance. The parent could not afford to be late and so would be that early. The gang had said 12.30, so it was unlikely that they'd risk showing themselves before then. He did not know how they planned to make their escape but he did not care. As long as he had the money and had made his escape, all would be well.

At last it was 12.15 a.m. He started the bike and tore out of the lane the short distance to the bin. He did not know that he had been seen and identified by crouching nearby police while he waited. Willie snatched the bag of money and roared quickly to his escape lane, while policemen rushed towards him from everywhere. Willie knew that without the lane he would have had no chance of escape.

The lane was empty as he roared down it, bouncing on the cobbles. He had just got to the far end when a police car blocked the exit. He looked back in shock to see armed police at the end of the lane he had come from.

"Hello, Willie," said Officer Hutchinson, who knew him well. "On the wrong side of the law this time, eh?" he remarked pleasantly.

Willie could not hide his anger and frustration. He swore loudly and for a long time as rough hands pulled him from the bike.

"Tut, tut!" said Officer Hutchinson, as if he'd never heard before the things Willie was saying. "Such language, Willie!"

Chapter Thirteen

The Second Ransom Demand

Willie had a great deal of trouble convincing the police that he was not in fact the kidnapper and that he'd found a copy of the ransom note. Fortunately for him, he eventually remembered that he had not thrown out what he'd found. The police experts checked it against the one sent to Graham and declared that it came from the same source, only with a little less detail. Also, although Willie could still have sent it, there were witnesses that he was recovering, on a friend's couch, from a heavy night of drinking on the morning the girls were kidnapped.

Willie was charged—after he had been properly cautioned—with "Obtaining Money on False Pretences" and "Avoiding Arrest". These were reasonably serious offences, but nothing anywhere near as serious as "Kidnapping", "False Imprisonment" and "Obtaining Money with Menaces" that faced the real kidnappers.

Everyone knew that it had to be the gang—but how could that be proved? They too appeared to have an alibi. They could be arrested on suspicion but, should they be unable to break them down, they would have to be released within twenty-four hours anyway. And what might happen to the girls in the meantime? What might the gang do to them after the police had released them? Would they consider the girls too dangerous to stay alive? Or were they already dead?

Graham and Natalie and Crispin and Marion were sick with worry. They had not fulfilled the gang's demands about 'no police'.

How would they and/or the girls pay for this? They had expected it to be all over by now and to have the girls safely home with the gang members caught. The gang had been too clever for them

It was with some sense of relief then, perhaps surprisingly, to get the second ransom note, even though the price had gone up to a million dollars. Loss of the money security for their future was one thing, unpleasant though that was. Loss of their beloved girls would be an absolute tragedy. Both families wondered whether they would survive that.

There was a prepaid mobile phone in the packet, and the delivery was made by the most commonly used courier company. The sender was a Mr H. L. D. Toogles. Marion snorted with frustration. "Held Two Girls!" she snarled.

The new ransom note read:

You stuffd up and we ought to just kill yore girls for not following instrctions.

We will give yous one more chance. This time, if yous tell the police we will realy kill them

We have put proof here that they are still alive For now.

Take this phone and follow instrctions carefully. Start in Belton near the supermarket on Wed night at 5.pm.

And the price is now one million. Get it right.

So the gang was going to start the run-down to the ransom drop on what was effectively home soil. Even if the police were to be around for the start of the process, which would have been extremely dangerous, how could they have kept track of what was clearly going to be a process of "Go here, now go there"?

The only possible way to find them would be by helicopter which could lead the fleeing gang to kill the girls.

The "proof" was a photograph of the girls looking miserable, standing in front of a hung white sheet, which therefore could have been anywhere, holding up the front page of a newspaper from the day before the delivery of the ransom note.

The photo both cheered and depressed the girls' parents. They were cheered by the thought that the girls were still alive but felt terrible about how bedraggled and unhappy they looked. They were aware that this did not guarantee their future safety—but it was a start.

Chapter Fourteen

The Ransom Chase

Graham, it was felt, was the one who should chase the gang's demands around. There was some debate about why the gang had asked for such an early start but Natalie suggested that this would be so that the early stages of the process could be observed by one of the gang members who would be less obvious with a crowd of late afternoon shoppers around. Any sudden movement by some person who followed Graham would be noted.

Graham (or whichever parent was going to hand over the ransom) was instructed to get around on a low-powered motor bike with a light helmet and without a visor so that the face was visible. The gang seemed to have thought of everything. Both the police and the parents were in despair. Was there any way they could be in control of the process?

Five o'clock came and Graham took the ransom and took up his place outside the supermarket, with the bag over his shoulder, and the bike nearby. He was pacing nervously to begin with and had to stop and control himself and stand reasonably still.

The phone went and Graham nearly dropped it in fright. He was shaking as he pressed the button to answer.

"He-e-llo", he said.

"Get a grip on ya'self", said a muffled voice, probably speaking through a folded cloth, like a handkerchief or a tea-towel, "If ya draw attention ta ya'self so people notice, all bets are off! Now get on ya bike and head out the road to Melbourne. Ya'll get more instructions five k's out where there's a bend and a farmhouse entrance with a small home-made blue post box fer the farm's letters. Be there in ten minutes.

"In it ya'll find another phone. Ditch that one in a rubbish bin so no one sees ya'."

Graham groaned inwardly. The phone he had had been rigged so that the police could listen to the conversation. Now even that possibility had gone. The place where the next phone would be found was out in the open and practically deserted. The farm owners would have collected their mail much earlier and would be getting ready to have their dinner, or perhaps have had it and were well settled in to an evening of television. Only Graham could approach the letter box and he would be watched to check that he was alone. It seemed his last chance was gone.

He reached the place with two minutes to spare. The phone was there and it rang as soon as he picked it up. "Right, yar a good boy," said the voice. "Now go up the road about three hundred metres and take the track across the paddock that goes at an angle to the right. About another kilometre away there's a track down to a gully. Go down into that gully where there's a lot a' trees along an old creek. Go inter them trees an' wait."

Graham got on to his bike and did as he was told. As he went into the clump of trees he was jumped and knocked to the ground. It was a heavy blow and he was dazed. Shady quickly gagged him and tied him up, after stripping off his clothes. A few minutes later the bike, with its rider and bag of ransom money, emerged out of the trees. It would have looked, from a distance, as if Graham was on his way, having got his next set of instructions. The gang appeared to have everything they wanted and to have escaped detection.

Chapter Fifteen

Second Escape Attempt

While this was going on the girls, still held in their reinforced prison, were in despair. Sarah looked hopelessly out the window at the farmer's dopey dog as it took a rat up to the farmhouse as a present for the old man. It seemed that it just collected things and left them at the back door.

"Hey, Emily!" shouted Sarah suddenly.

Emily looked up out of her red-rimmed eyes.

"You don't have to shout, she said crossly. "It's not as if I'm far away!"

"Have you noticed that farmer's dog?"

"Course I have," said Emily. "It just goes up and down to the farmhouse with something in its stupid mouth."

Suddenly, Emily could see where Sarah was coming from. She sprang to her feet. "What can we give it to take up to the farmer? It can't be something like a sneaker, 'cos that could have come from anywhere and anyone." She was getting excited now. "Why not a fair bit of our school dress? They've had it anyway, so it's no loss."

She tore at her dress and ripped a large chunk off and screwed it up into a ball. When the dog came back she called it over. She'd heard in the distance the old farmer call out to the dog from time to time. They'd both screamed out to him without getting any response. The dog was called "Fergie'.

The girls had thought this was strange, as the dog was obviously (too obviously, they'd have said) male. The only 'Fergie' they knew of was Sarah Ferguson, now estranged from the British royal family, but often in the news, a feisty lady with fiery red hair. This dog was greyish with black paws. It took them some time to realise that this was the colour of the farmer's precious Ferguson tractor.

After they had been calling for some time, eventually the dog came up to the window, its tongue hanging from its slobbering mouth.

"Good boy," said Emily, throwing her piece of dress out the window. The dog picked it up, probably attracted by the obvious odour that was by now part of their clothes. Looking pleased with itself, it headed off back to the farmhouse, while the girls hugged each other in renewed hope.

"What if the farmer doesn't come out and get it?" asked Sarah.

"What if he does and he doesn't know what it is or wonder where it's come from?" asked Emily.

As it happened, the old farmer, who was mostly deaf and blind, had begun to wonder whether something was going on out the back of his place. A few nights back, he'd seen what he thought was a light in his shed, but when he went out to check, he saw nothing as he approached it. One-Shot was there and, hearing the farmer's back door bang, had quickly turned off the light he'd carelessly put on at a time when the old man would still be up.

To One-Shot's relief, the old man had turned and gone back to his house, scratching his head as he went, thinking he must have imagined it and not wanting to go into a dark shed where he could trip and possibly break his hip. If he did he'd be left helpless out there in the dark. He knew that he was pushing his luck staying on the farm and he wasn't prepared to take the risk.

Another time, when the girls had been screaming their lungs out, he thought he'd heard a noise but he couldn't be sure and had again done nothing. Now his dog had brought him what was clearly a chunk of school dress. He always listened to an old radio that he held to his ear with the sound up. He knew that there had been a kidnap of girls in the area and this was too much of a coincidence to be ignored.

Bravely, he got out his old shotgun and walked slowly into his back yard. He would have to risk it. Probably what he'd find would be the bodies of the two girls. But he had to check.

When he got into the shed he called out. "Is anyone there?-" he croaked in a shaky voice.

"Yes!!" shrieked both girls together.

"Anyone else?" asked the farmer anxiously, knowing that he would make an easy target, despite the shotgun.

"No!" shrieked the girls.

The gang were off busy with the details of the ransom collection. It took all three of them. Shelly had hidden in old deserted legal office about half a block from the supermarket entrance. She used binoculars to check what Graham was doing.

One-Shot was hiding in long grass watching Graham at the farm gate. He needed to be sure Graham was following directions. Shady, as we already know, was waiting for Graham in the gully. The girls would be safe in their farm prison. They were left for quite long stretches anyway and they could surely be left a little longer.

Chapter Sixteen

The End of the Road

When the farmer knew that the girls were there, that they were alive, and that the gang was elsewhere, he became quite brave. "Hang on, girls," he called. "I'll get you out!" He soon found that there was a padlock between him and the girls.

"Stand back over in the corner near the churn," he called out. With a deafening roar, the shotgun blasted the lock off. The relieved girls rushed out and hugged him.

"Hang on, hang on," he mumbled in embarrassment. "We need to ring he police on this one".

Without waiting to be invited, the girls dashed past him towards the house. They rushed in the back door and looked around for the phone, which they found in the kitchen, near to the old wood stove but far enough away not to suffer from the heat.

Sarah was there first. She rang 000 and it seemed to be an age before she was put through to the police.

"Hello," she said excitedly, "We are the girls who were kidnapped. Or at least I am, the person speaking", she said, feeling stupid or awkward with trying to get it out and make it accurate at the same time. "And my friend Emily is here too."

"My God," said the voice at the other end of the phone. "Where are you?"

"Where are we?" asked both girls together. The farmer, who had come up from the shed more slowly, told them and with huge excitement, the voice at the other end was shouting to the people around him. Another voice came on and told them to stay put. Help was on its way.

When the gang came back with the ransom money to decide what to do with the girls, they would find, if they were quick, the farmer with his newly reloaded shotgun. Fairly soon afterwards there would be armed police from a "paddy wagon", a vehicle designed to carry suspects and criminals safely to police stations or gaols. If the police were quicker than the criminals, the farmer suggested, this vehicle could be discreetly hidden from sight behind an old haystack. It should not be obviously around to arouse the suspicions of the gang who would turn and run if they saw police there

Superintendent Walker himself decided to lead the police team to the farm. There were two reasons for this. In the first place, the case had become such a dramatic and high-profile one that he would need to be the one to report to the press and he wanted to report accurately about exactly how it had been. Secondly, he decided, wisely, that he did not want Officer Hutchinson to have to face the parents alone. With some justification, they would still be very angry that his mistake had made the kidnap possible.

He nevertheless took "Hutchie" with him. The man needed to face the situation and perhaps gain some healing and confidence from the way it had turned out successfully.

The Superintendent took a grim pleasure from the fact that the only way that officer could get to the farm would be in the back of the "Paddy Wagon, as the front seat would be taken up by him and the driver" He did not want too many police vehicles there. Walker was also making the point—none too subtly—that Hutchinson had been guilty of 'criminal' neglect.

Walker wanted to wait for them in the shed where the girls had been imprisoned, so there could be absolutely no mistake about who was responsible. Besides which, in the unlikely event of a repeat of a failure to caution them, he would do it himself.

And so it was that when the gang members came sneaking across the paddocks to the shed, they found Walker, Hutchinson and another armed policeman, the driver, waiting for them. Walker had activated an alarm that would bring another car, full of armed policemen, to the farm. They had been waiting in the next farm and were quickly on the spot.

Seeing the waiting police, One-Shot pulled out his gun, only to find himself facing two heavily armed police with automatic weapons poised.

"Don't even think about it, One-Shot!" said Walker, in the best tradition of police dramas. He was tempted to say instead, like Clint Eastwood in *Dirty Harry,* "Go ahead; make my day," but he realized that this was, in fact, a serious and solemn moment, so he resisted.

Walker was pleased to see the look of satisfaction on Officer Hutchinson's face as he ordered the three gang members to turn around and be handcuffed. One-Shot was cursing loudly; Shelly was there so the girls' fate could be spelt out to them. She'd decided that it was too dangerous for them to stay alive. She looked daggers at the other two. They had been the ones responsible for keeping the girls secure. Shady was quiet, almost as if he was simply glad it was all over

He had not wanted the girls to be killed but the other two had outvoted him. He could see why it would be safer, but he rather liked them and admired their spirit, especially when he saw what they had done to escape the first time.

"OK, Hutchinson," said Walker, "Got anything to say?"

"Yes, sir," said Hutchinson eagerly." I am charging the three of you with Kidnapping, with False Imprisonment, with Demanding Money with Menaces and with being in the Possession of Ransom Money. I need to warn you that you do not have to say anything . . ." he added, looking meaningfully at Walker, "But anything you do say may be written down and used in evidence against you . . . ."

Hutchinson's voice droned on. This time he was going to do it properly. He ended with, "And there may be further charges to follow"

"Well done, Hutchinson," approved Walker. "That should do it nicely. And I'm witness to what you've said."

One-Shot cursed more loudly until, Walker advised Hutchinson to take "restraining action". This he did with some force, leaving One-Shot to squeal loudly about "police brutality", a complaint that did little to help him as he was bundled into the back of the "Paddy Wagon"

Shady might once have been tempted to assist his partner in crime but he was still angry at One-Shot's suggestion, made on their way back to the farm—and supported by Shelly—that the girls would have to be "disposed of". Their continued existence, the two said, threatened the safety of them all. Shady did not hold with any more severe form of violence against children than he had already shown; and had had told them so in no uncertain terms. When One-Shot gave Shelly a meaningful glance, Shady knew that he too would be considered disposable and had determined to disarm One-Shot as soon as they reached the farm.

The police presence made this unnecessary but One-Shot's attitude would mean that the man who had previously protected him in prison was entirely unlikely to do so this next time.

Chapter Seventeen

Another Reunion

The girls' families were beside themselves with joy as soon as they knew that their precious girls were safe. While it was nice to know that the ransom was to be returned, for the moment, at least, this was not a concern. All four wept openly with relief but they asked the police to return the girls to them. They did not trust themselves to drive safely to collect them.

This was done promptly by Walker himself and another officer, it having been decided that it would be better for Hutchinson to stay well away from the parents' anger. While all declared the outcome "a good result" it was painfully obvious that this owed more to the ingenuity of the girls themselves than to the police.

The girls were equally delighted to see their parents. Crispin was still inclined to blame Graham for lack of his duty of care, but the other three—and the girls themselves—quickly made it clear that it was not fair. The girls had insisted that they would be safe on the bus, Natalie pointed out that had she left for town earlier, she would have seen the kidnap, which would probably have frightened them off, so perhaps it was her fault anyway.

All blamed Officer Hutchinson but, as Marion pointed out, being human meant that you made mistakes. Hutchinson had acted quickly to stop the gang escaping when the girls had banged on the boot after the first kidnap, so he could be thanked for this just as reasonably as be blamed for his failure to caution.

All declared their need for a holiday. The girls wanted Disney Land; the parents would have preferred a Fijian island or the Italian Lakes or the Cinque Terra. It was the wise Marion who said that if they were going to holiday they might as well do it properly and join teenage tastes with adult pleasure. Why not Paris? Apart from its usual attractions there was a Disney Land nearby.

So Paris it was.